It was a wild night. After all the disappointments of the day, after the cartoon shows and the brewskis, my friends went a little crazy. They played loud music and danced with wide, sinuous motions. They passed around funny cigarettes and ate strawberry yoyogurt. But the party was a little too hysterical. Mostly, I sat in a corner of the room watching these unfamiliar tribal dances. Giggling, Flopsie and Mopsie came over to my corner and one of them sat on either side of me. They began to cuddle with me.

I lost track of the time, and the next thing I knew Flopsie and Mopsie were sitting back on their heels giggling and pointing at the place between my legs. I looked down and saw that my pants were around my ankles. Flopsie called her friend over.

"Cowabunga," she said, "Is that how they hang in Bay City?"

"Hang what?" I said. I felt myself falling sideways but was asleep before I hit the floor.

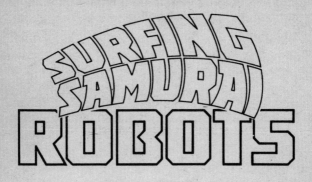

SURFING SAMURAI ROBOTS

Mel Gilden

LYNX BOOKS
New York

Special thanks to Andrea Brown
and Mary Higgins

SURFING SAMURAI ROBOTS

ISBN: 1-55802-001-2

First Printing/ August 1988

This book is published by Lynx Books, a division of Lynx Communications, Inc., 41 Madison Avenue, New York, New York, 10010. The name ''Lynx'' together with the logotype consisting of a stylized head of a lynx is a trademark of Lynx Communications, Inc.

Cover art by David Dorman
Cover design by Alex Jay
Edited by David M. Harris

Printed in the United States of America

0 9 8 7 6 5 4 3 2 1

For
Ms. Laurie:
Woman of Mystery

CONTENTS

Introduction

I was a long way from T'toom.

The computers did most of the work aboard my ship, the *Philip Marlowe*, and I had plenty of leisure in which to think about how I had come to be there, miles above an obscure planet, and falling toward its biggest ocean.

T'toom was a nice place, and you would absolutely want to live there. I did, anyway, for a long time.

When I first heard the signals the AW–OL guys were pulling in with their backyard rig, I was working for T'toom Gravitational Products, the family business Grampa Zamp had started when he was about my age.

I was running slaberingeo ear spines through a vat of fixer, so that the anti-gravity stuff covering the spines wouldn't rot. I grew up to hate slaberingeo spines. They smelled bad, and they left behind tiny itchy hairs that you could never get rid of entirely, no matter how much you washed.

I had stopped to enjoy a thorough and useless scratch when my radio played a recording of the first signal AW–OL received. The eerie sounds didn't make any sense to me then. But like a lot of people, I never forgot where I was when I heard them.

AW–OL meant Alien Worlds–Overhearing Life. These guys had aimed a big dish at the sky, trying to listen in on conversations they suspected the big kids were having just among themselves at the other end of the galaxy. No one was more surprised than they when they actually heard something.

As more broadcasts came in, scientists accumulated enough of a sample that they were able to decode them. In a few years, everybody was learning English. "Talking like an Earthman" became as common as household ooze or slaberingeo spines. All the best people did it at parties. English became the international language of trade and diplomacy. I took some classes, too, so as not to be left out.

We didn't know what Earthpeople looked like, though everybody had an opinion. Magazines were full of artists' conceptions. According to them, Earthpeople were just like Toomlers, but with more arms and funny things on the sides of their heads that collected sound—things Earthpeople on the radio called ears. The pictures were interesting but ultimately pointless. There was no way to know for sure.

That first broadcast became famous, not just because it was first, but because it terrified everybody on T'toom. What we heard was that some planet called Earth was being invaded by some other planet called Mars. Mars was doing pretty well. It was possible that when Mars finished with Earth, T'toom would be next.

The AW–OL guys eventually figured out that the invasion of Earth by Mars was a fake, written by Howard Koch and performed by Orson Welles and the Mercury Theater.

We had theater on T'toom, but nothing like this.

Even before the AW–OL guys had figured this out, American radio became all the rage. I listened too, but I didn't really get excited until I heard *The Adventures of Philip Marlowe* for the first time.

Marlowe was a rough, tough detective who took no lip from anyone. I imagined I looked a lot like him. I wanted to look more like him, but nobody on T'toom knew any more about trench coats or fedoras than they did about Earthpeople.

My work with T'toom Gravitational Products began to suffer. All I could think about was Philip Marlowe and the babes who fell for him, and the corrupt cops and big money and gats and heaters. *A man with a gun entered the room. Bang! A shot rang out! Marlowe dodged just in time!* I loved that stuff.

I knew that Philip Marlowe was just as big a fake as Orson Welles's Martians. After all, he was played by an actor named Van Heflin. And he always solved his cases in exactly the same amount of time. That seemed unlikely in reality. But I didn't care about any of this. Marlowe himself might be a fake, but there had to be guys on Earth like him. I didn't think you could imagine a guy like Marlowe out of nowhere.

Finally, my dad called me into the office. It was a new office, just oozed, and the walls glistened a wet orange. Dad said, "Zoot, your mind isn't on your work." He actually spoke English. We all did, mostly. Our local language, Gomkrix, was just for peons.

I looked at the floor. "Yes, sir."

"What's the problem?"

For a moment I didn't know what to say. Then I decided, what the Durf, I'd tell him everything. Maybe he'd understand. My hopes were not very high.

As I spoke, Dad's nose twitched, showing how upset he was about what I was telling him. The more I talked, the faster it twitched. But the twitching stopped when I told him I wanted to go to Earth. Few things had frightened me as much as Dad's motionless nose.

Dad didn't say anything for a moment. Then he said, "You want to go to Earth and be a detective like Philip Marlowe." He sounded as if he couldn't believe that was actually what I'd told him. He spoke in a clear dramatic voice, just like somebody on the radio.

"Yes, sir."

"The family business is good enough for me and your Grampa Zamp. I thought it might be good enough for you too."

"It's fine, sir. It's just that I would like to try some other things before I settle down."

His nose twitched a little, encouraging me. He said, "How would you get to Earth?"

"I thought I'd buy a secondhand sneeve." A sneeve was a round interstellar ship named after a round animal that spun through the air from tree to tree.

"With what would you buy this sneeve?"

Dad had certainly put his finger right where it hurt. I said, "I thought you might loan me the money."

"When would you pay it back?"

"When I came back to T'toom, I'd work for free."

"That's unlikely." He paused. I was afraid he'd stopped altogether. I was on the edge of backing out the door, taking my dreams of hot babes and cold gats with me. Dad looked up, seemed surprised to see I was still there. He said, "You know that nobody from T'toom has ever actually landed on Earth."

"I know that, Dad, but they've mapped the whole

thing from the air. I have an idea where I want to land."

"If the radio is any indicator, civilization on Earth is not very civilized. Nobody has landed on Earth because nobody wants to."

"Yes, sir. But they need me."

I'd never said that before. Never even thought it. But now that it had escaped from my mouth, I knew it was true. Those poor goons on Earth needed me. I could clean up their messes. Just like Philip Marlowe. *Blam! Blam! The Chevy* (What was a Chevy?) *roared away, tires squealing! Marlowe was tired, but he had to go on. Enough guys get away with murder, pretty soon, everybody's doing it.*

"I doubt that," Dad said. "Still, you're no good to me as you are. Maybe this is one way for you to get this private detective stuff out of your system."

I could feel both my hearts pumping hard, making the veins in my face throb.

"Go find a good sneeve. I'll pay for it. But you have to promise to be careful when you get to Earth."

He knew as well as I did that being careful on a planet like Earth would consist mainly of not going there at all. Once I landed, all bets were off. From the radio broadcasts, I had a general idea what to expect on Earth, but beyond that, anything was possible. Anything.

Dad said no more about it, and neither did I. I suppose he hoped that the danger of going to Earth would sink in at last, or something. And it almost did. I kept finding excuses not to go hunting for a sneeve.

Then one day, Grampa Zamp hobbled over to where I was taking down spines from a curing rack and said, "How's the search for the sneeve coming?"

I shrugged, unaccountably feeling guilty.

Grampa Zamp chuckled and said, "You remind me of myself at your age. Going to Earth was not on my list of things to do, but only because we hadn't yet received our first transmission. I wish I could go with you." He shook his head, then lifted his hat to fix me with a steely eye. I imagined the gangsters that Marlowe went up against looked like that. He said, "You *are* going, aren't you?"

"Oh, sure," I said.

So, I found a good secondhand sneeve, and my dad paid for it over my mom's objections. Grampa Zamp just chuckled and rubbed my nose to show that he was proud of me. When we weren't working for the company, he helped me plot out my landing place and what I would do after I came down. I never felt so close to Grampa Zamp, and I thought about staying on T'toom. But I knew that wasn't possible. If I stayed, Grampa Zamp would probably never speak to me again.

When the day came for me to go, I felt about as stupid as a slaberingeo, but I climbed into my sneeve and took off.

The trip didn't take long. I ate and slept, but mostly I thought and played recordings I'd made of *The Adventures of Philip Marlowe.*

Now, I was only miles above an obscure planet called Earth, and falling toward its biggest ocean—the Pacific Ocean, if the radio could be believed.

I dove through the atmosphere, and when my sneeve sliced into the ocean, first the water was green, and then blue, and then darker till it was almost black. Creatures swam around me, not even curious. Fish, I thought. When I judged I was deep enough, I started the pulsator and moved toward the shore, leaving a wake of interference waves behind me.

I admit it: I was excited. When the ship stopped, I stood before the airlock screw for a moment trying to remember what I was doing here. I could still turn around and go home. Sure. In a pig's eye. Durf, I didn't even know what a pig was.

I cycled the airlock screw, and it twisted me out into cold salty water. I took my bearings and swam toward the beach, where creatures leaped after a thing that looked like a sneeve. Sneeves? Here? This was Earth! There weren't even any trees!

Soon the water was shallow enough that I could feel my feet touch the sandy bottom. I walked out of the water, my clothes dripping wet. The Earthpeople were so busy with their sneeve that they didn't even notice me.

I was busy too. Busy staring.

CHAPTER 1
'Bu

Earthpeople were taller than I had expected. And pinker. Toomlers tend to run from pure white to a soft, earthy brown. Pink was a surprise. And their faces were *real* different. I could see they'd take some getting used to. If you mashed a Toomler face flat, it might look like one of these. There were those big eyes, and a mouth with a red ring around it, and what I took to be a nose. The nose was sort of a pimple in the middle of each face, unlike the nose on a Toomler, which, for all practical purposes, *is* the face.

And instead of the treated tree sap we wear, they wore tubes of soft stuff in many colorful patterns. Unless, of course, the tubes and patterns were part of their bodies.

I walked up the wet sand onto the dry stuff and stopped. The Earthpeople on the beach laughed as they sailed the sneeve to each other. Nobody ever missed. They were good. I wondered if flinging the ol' sneeve was actually a profession on Earth.

Suddenly, the sneeve-thing spun at me. Reflexively, I reached up and pulled it out of the sky. The thing they were throwing wasn't really a sneeve, of course. It was made of stiff red stuff with raised patterns all over it, some of which may have been writing.

The Earthpeople saw me now. They watched me carefully but kept backing away, as if they thought I was a slaberingeo. I held up the sneeve in one hand, and an open palm with the other. I hoped the empty palm would be the universal sign that I wasn't carrying a weapon, and I said, "I'm not heeled, if that's what you're worried about, sweethearts."

"Cowabunga!" more than one of them cried. "It talks English!"

Their astonishment was fair enough, considering how physically different I was from them. They may have even guessed that I wasn't from Earth. Guessed? Durf, if they weren't certain of it, I was dealing with the wrong dominant race. Grampa Zamp and I had discussed the problem posed by my origin and decided the direct approach would be best. Just brazen the situation out. I said, "That seems to make two of us."

More astonishment among the masses. I threw the sneeve at one of the Earthpeople, a very tall one wearing vibrant blue tubes. The Earthperson caught it easily and held it awkwardly, uncertain whether to throw it back or not.

"Look," I said, "you folks seem to be laboring under the misconception that I'm something special."

"Dig that bitchen schnoz," one of them said. The rest laughed, but as far as I could tell, it was nervous laughter. It was just something to do until the shock went away.

I said, "I have to explain this all the time. I was born funny."

"You mean a birth defect?" the Earthperson holding the sneeve said.

Birth defect? It had a nice ring to it. I could use that phrase. "Yes," I said, "a birth defect."

"Pretty aggro defect," the man who had commented on my schnoz said. He thought he was funnier than Fred Allen. But he knew a lot of words I'd never heard on the radio. Evidently, there was a lot more to English than "Stick 'em up."

"Maybe his mother took something in the sixties," another of them said. This one had a vaguely different shape from the comedian or the one holding the sneeve. A female? Her hair was red and hung to her shoulders.

"Good guess," I said, wondering what the sixties were.

"Rip it, Thumper," the comedian called.

Thumper considered for a moment, and then threw the sneeve to me. I caught it, and threw it to someone else. Pretty soon, we were all throwing the sneeve around together as if we'd been doing it all our lives, just one big happy family.

When Thumper brushed back his hair with a hand, I could see flaps growing on either side of his head. Those must be ears. Very fancy. Now that I'd seen his, I noticed that most of the others had ears too. It was hard to tell about some of them, their hair was so long.

The sun was going down. It looked a lot like T'toom's sun going down from T'toom. I felt homesick and threw the sneeve harder, trying to make the feeling go away. But homesickness stuck like house ooze that had been left out too long.

I was homesick, and there was nothing to do about it but make Earth my home. If I went back to T'toom now, Grampa Zamp would never speak to me again, and everywhere I went, I'd be the guy who failed.

Besides, these Earth folks needed me. I had to remember that. If the radio broadcasts were any indication, there was enough crime to support one more private eye.

Pretty soon, the air turned cool and the Earthpeople moved up the beach to a pile of wood. Nobody objected when I fell in line. I love a parade.

They lit a fire using small sticks they snicked against paper packets. The fire roared and crackled and gave off an unusual, but not unpleasant, smell. Thumper threw a metal grid onto the fire and on top of that laid out lumps of flesh. Were they about to eat, or was this some ritual connected with sneeve-throwing? I hoped it was food. I'd been living on food processed by my ship from my own waste. Disgusting, but fairly efficient. A wonderful smell filled the air.

"Hey! Boss!" Thumper commented. "I love chicken, don't you?" He looked at me expectantly. Was this a trick question?

"What's not to love?" I said.

That seemed to satisfy him, and he energetically poked the chicken with a long sharp stick.

Somebody threw a towel around me. But it wasn't like a Toomler towel. It seemed to be made from soft stuff, like Earth clothes. In any case, I was grateful for it because a wind was blowing off the ocean. It was a cold wind, but it was not blowing hard. It acted as if it were not sure it wanted to explore anything so dry as a continent. A good thought. That wind would have liked T'toom.

We sat around the fire warming our hands. Our hands were similar, anyway. I stared into the fire while the chicken popped and smoked. In the flames I imagined I could see abo forests and slaberingeos. I wondered what the Earthpeople around me saw.

The red-headed female came down the beach gripping her side of a white box by a handle. Holding the handle on the other side was another red-headed female who looked very much like her. Some animals on T'toom had twins, but never Toomlers. I kept my prejudices to myself.

An Earthman pulled two white cylinders from among ice cubes in the white box. He wore yellow tubes on his legs, and no tubes at all on his upper body. His upper body had a lot of curly golden hair on it. More hair hung from his head.

Most of the others grabbed cylinders too, and with a motion I did not quite catch, opened them and poured whatever was inside down their throats.

The guy in the yellow tubes handed one of the cylinders to me. "Have a brewski," he said.

The cylinder was cold, of course, and made of metal. I stood there like a slaberingeo, with the cylinder in my hand but not sure what to do with it. The guy in yellow opened his cylinder and drank from it. I made a couple of tries to work the lever on top of the metal can before he grabbed it away from me and, slowly this time, pulled back the lever to make a hole appear in the can's top.

The comedian said, "A guy who can't handle a pop-top must have *some* birth defect."

The moment of truth. What, exactly, was a brewski? Earthmen drank it, but could I? I might be poisoning myself. End of adventure. But, Durf, I was tired of eating my own reconstituted waste. Besides, I'd have to eat Earth food eventually.

I couldn't fit the can under the end of my nose, so I sipped a little through the side of my mouth. I coughed and sputtered yellow liquid onto the sand where it fizzed for a moment, then sank in. I don't know if the stuff was poisonous, but it smelled like abo sap and tasted like spine fixer. For the first time, I wondered if I should not have stayed home.

My friend took the can away from me and handed it to one of his friends. With a motion like a dancer, he folded his legs and sank to the sand. "You're not from around here, are you?"

"Not exactly," I said, still trying to catch my breath. "Where exactly am I?"

" 'Bu," said the comedian.

"Malibu," said my friend in the yellow tubes. "Malibu, California. Good ol' U.S. of A." He fixed me with a hard look. "Planet Earth." He said that last as if it meant something special. His friends were all looking at me. I was not comfortable.

I said, "Give that man ten silver dollars."

"What about you?" the comedian said.

"The name's Zoot, uh, Marlowe," I said.

"Where are you from, Zoot Marlowe?" the comedian said, as if he wouldn't believe whatever I told him.

"Bay City," I said.

"Never heard of it."

"It's up the coast," I said. "On the Planet Earth."

All the Earthmen laughed. We were having a good time just sitting around a fire, talking radio dialogue to each other.

"This is Captain Hook," my friend said, gesturing

at the comedian with his white can. "I'm Whipper Will."

"Of Malibu."

"Right," Captain Hook said.

Whipper Will gestured at each of his friends with his brewski. "That's Hanger and Bingo over there with Thumper and Mustard. The two cute redheads are Mopsie and Flopsie."

I nodded.

"The chicken's done," Thumper said.

There wasn't much conversation after that, and what there was was mostly incomprehensible to me. Oh, it was English all right, but spined with words I'd never heard before. I concentrated on the chicken. I don't know what it had been when it was alive, but dead, it was pretty good. Certainly an improvement on recycled excrement.

It made me thirsty enough to try another brewski. Maybe the stuff took some getting used to. It seemed to be a popular drink, at least among these folks on the beach. It was a little less awful each time I took a sip. I was getting pretty good at drinking it now, a champ. I could drink without spilling.

As I drank, concentrating became harder. Everything became more real, yet mattered less. Very strange. I wondered if there were something in the air. I finished my chicken and my brewski at about the same time. I said, "Could I have another one of these?" I held up the empty can and squeezed it. It wrinkled and held a dent. Hanger saw what I had done and laughed.

My voice did not sound right to me, and my tongue did not fit comfortably in my mouth. I didn't know what was going on, but I was enjoying it. I didn't care, anyway.

"Sure," Captain Hook said. He produced a can from somewhere and handed it to me. I knew how to open the can now, but my fingers kept slipping off the little lever. "Let me help," Captain Hook said. He opened the can and it sprayed him with foam. "Cowabunga!" he cried and quickly set the can on the sand. Brewski ran down the sides of the can. A few seconds later, the show was over, and I picked it up.

"Cowabunga," I said and knocked back a big gulp. I was amazed how good this stuff tasted after I'd been drinking it for a while. All around me, my friends were pairing off. As far as I could tell, each pair consisted of a male and a female. The pairs seemed to go into convulsions. Maybe I ought to do something to help them, but nobody else seemed upset. They churned the sand pretty good.

Whipper Will sat down beside me again. When had he left? I didn't know. Bingo watched us from across the fire. Whipper Will said, "Hi there, bro'. Did you get enough to eat?"

"Plenty," I said. I think I said "plenty." I wasn't very good with words this evening.

He looked at the sky. I looked up too. The bowl was absolutely black and filled with stars. I tried for a moment to find T'toom's sun but gave up. Focusing was difficult. Besides, the *Philip Marlowe*'s computer knew a lot more about astrogation than I did.

"You know," Whipper Will said, "nobody's ever going to believe that story about birth defects."

"No?"

"No."

"Why not?"

"For one thing, your case was never in the papers. The papers are stoked on freaks. For another, there are just too many things you don't know."

"Like how to open a brewski," I said. But it wasn't my voice. I was on automatic. Someone deep inside me was running things.

"For one, yes."

"Most of your friends bought it."

"My friends are not very analytical. Besides, they're pushovers for somebody who knows how to throw a Frisbee."

"Frisbee?"

"The round plastic thing."

I knew he meant the sneeve, but I didn't tell him that. I just said, "Ah."

"So," he said, "which of those stars are you from?"

"You may not believe this, but your guess is as good as mine. Better, if you know anything about astronomy."

"OK. Let's try this: How do you come to speak English?"

"Radio broadcasts."

Whipper Will nodded. We looked at the sky for a while. He said, "Why are you here?"

"You need help."

"Me?"

"You. All of you."

"We need help? I saw that movie."

"What's a movie?"

Whipper Will laughed softly. He said, "*Who* needs help?"

I closed my eyes. Storms of blackness roared be-

hind them. I opened my eyes. Nothing had changed.
I said, "Ever hear of Philip Marlowe?"

"Sure."

"He's my hero."

Whipper Will nodded again. I closed my eyes. The
blackness roared around me, and this time sucked me
in.

CHAPTER 2
Surf's Up!

The next thing I knew, light was shining in my eyes. I blinked and opened them, but closed them quickly and groaned. I didn't feel well. If only the room would stop tumbling, I might have an even chance of feeling better.

What had done this terrible thing to me? Was it the chicken? The brewski? The air? Something I knew nothing about? I didn't know, but if I was going to make a habit of getting up in the morning feeling like the sludge at the bottom of a spine vat, I was going home. I'd rather face Grampa Zamp.

Sound was coming from somewhere not far away. Organized tones with a beat. Maybe it was music. The point is, it kept poking my head like a stiff, bony finger. The music stopped abruptly, and a man began to talk about something called a free tune-up. His voice was not an improvement on the music.

I sat up, but too quickly, because I left my head where it had been. I fell back to join it and groaned again.

A voice said, "I don't know how you're supposed

to look in the morning, but if *I* looked like that, I'd feel awful."

I opened my eyes a slit and saw Whipper Will standing over me with a bowl. I tried to smile the way I'd seen the Earthpeople smile the day before. The fact that I hadn't had much practice did not make doing it any easier.

Just as an experiment, I loosened my tongue and said, "Beauty isn't everything." I sounded OK. Maybe I'd live. Too bad.

"Here," said Whipper Will. "Have some of this."

He grabbed an arm and pulled me to a sitting position. I grabbed my head to keep it from rolling across the floor. It was too late to grab my stomach. It had gone back to T'toom without me, leaving a big sick void.

I seemed to be sitting on a padded platform in a room crowded with things I could not identify. I couldn't be sure because my eyes refused to focus, even when I could get them to open. But the smells weren't so easy to ignore. The mix of brewski and other things in the air was not unpleasant, but it was as alien as anything Orson Welles had ever invented.

Whipper Will thrust the cold bowl into my hands and said, "Eat this. It'll make you feel better."

"What is it?"

"Yoyogurt. Strawberry."

"Absolutely no help at all."

"Eat it."

"I might as well. If it kills me, my head will stop throbbing." Sticking out of the pink stuff in the bowl was a shiny metal stick. I ignored it and lifted a little yoyogurt to my mouth on a finger. It had an odd flavor—sweet and sour at once. But it tasted clean, a nice change from the dry rot in my mouth. It dropped into the empty space where my stomach had been and spread waves of comfort. I tried a little more. My stomach returned to see what was up, liked what it saw, and stayed. I began to hum a tune I hadn't even thought of since I was a kid.

"Don't you have spoons in Bay City?" Whipper Will said.

"Spoons?"

He lifted the metal stick with a mound of yoyogurt at the business end. He said, "Here comes the airplane," and swooped the spoon toward my mouth.

"What?"

He shook his head and said, "Open your mouth."

I opened up, and he fed me a spoonful of yoyogurt. I managed to feed myself after that. It was easy for an intelligent guy like me. He said, "You finish all that and I'll be back soon with a surprise." He walked out of the room.

Terrific. That was exactly what I needed. Another surprise.

I ate everything in the bowl and wanted more. Truth was, it was pretty good stuff. My head was almost its normal size and in no danger of going off by itself. My stomach had moved in a little furniture and was feeling comfortable. I've felt better, but not long before, I'd felt much worse. This wasn't so bad. I could handle this.

I sat on the padded platform for a while, enjoying the sensations of an alien planet and of a reasonably healthy body. From across the room, a big gray-green eye stared at me from its box. Everything in the room had a rainbow around it. I moved my hand in front of my face the way a baby might, fascinated at the changing colors. If I'd had any sense, I'd have been frightened. But the yoyogurt had relaxed me to the point where there was nothing to be afraid of. Nothing anywhere in the universe. I should have been frightened by that too.

The ocean crashed into the beach again and again, always there behind the music and talk. Its salty smell wafted through the room like a ghost of the ocean, never quite replacing the smell of brewski and of the room itself.

Obviously, Earthpeople did not build their buildings out of ooze, the way we did on T'toom. The walls were flat and didn't glisten. They were nearly the same color as I was, not quite white.

Hanging from them were big colorful pictures of Earthpeople standing on water. The radio had never mentioned that Earthpeople could do that. Maybe they didn't like to talk about it for religious reasons. Taboos are funny things.

Next to me on the platform were some folded sheets. I unfolded a stack of them with a rattling sound. Each sheet was covered with black marks that were probably writing and a picture or two of Earthpeople going about their business. Most of them had a lot more tubes on than my friends. And less hair. More of these white sheets were in untidy piles on the floor. Among them were piles of similar things—more black marks—but on shiny paper with colored pictures. Most of the pictures showed Earthpeople walking on water.

The rainbows made everything look not quite real. That fit. I wasn't feeling very real myself. Still, I tried to think about this walking-on-water stuff. It was obviously important.

At the best of times, thinking was a dangerous activity, and I was far from being at my best. I had so many questions about what I would do next, and how, that I didn't know where to begin. Questions swirled in my head like geometric solids, showing first one side, and then another, none of them suggesting anything.

The sticky bowl became a nuisance. I shifted it from hand to hand and finally put it on the platform beside me. The spoon rattled against it. The bowl and spoon didn't look good there, despite the rainbows. Getting rid of the bowl and spoon became very important for me. But it had to be done right. Very important.

I giggled and tried standing up. On the second attempt I was successful. What a guy. I picked up the empty bowl and followed the music.

Instead of being all rooms, the way a Toomler building was, this Earth building had tunnels leading from one room to another. I weaved along a tunnel and came out in a room where the music was very loud. This one was even brighter than the one I'd left, but I was a tough guy. I could stand it now. I'd eaten my yoyogurt.

The blue walls were covered with something that looked like Toomler house gelatin, but was hard to the touch. Where there wasn't something sitting on them, I could see the counter tops were covered with squares of the same stuff. In the center of one of the counters was a deep indentation that had a small mountain of dirty dishes in it. I reached up and put my bowl on top of the stack, wondering what would happen when the stack got high enough.

In one corner of the room was a small box that

looked as if it were made out of the same stuff as the Frisbee. The music blared out of it. I reached through the rainbows, picked up the box, and turned it over, not affecting the music at all. There was a good chance that this was what a radio looked like on Earth.

I turned one of the dials, hoping to find a drama like the ones I'd listened to at home—maybe even an adventure of Philip Marlowe. No luck. I got more people talking, all right, but they sounded as if they were making the words up as they went along. Boring words, at least to a stranger like myself. I hadn't the patience to make sense of them.

There was more music too. No Marlowe. No invasion from Mars. Maybe this thing wasn't a radio after all. I tried the other knob, and the sound got louder. I quickly turned the knob the other way and made the radio whisper. This seemed to be an improvement, so I left it that way.

Through big windows, I could see Earthpeople—each of them wearing tubes of one kind or another—walking along a wide black path between the house and the beach. Hair length seemed to be a matter of personal taste. A pair of females, purple tubes tight against their bodies, slid by on shoes that had wheels on the bottom.

Beyond the black band, the ocean rose and fell and hurried up the beach as if it had an appointment, and the sand spread out like a big yellow-brown animal sleeping in the sun.

The sun was very bright and harsh and fell from a cloudless blue sky as hard as diamonds. I had no idea what a diamond was, but in the radio broadcasts they were always hard and shiny and worth somebody's life to have around.

Out on the water, Earthpeople were walking around. I watched closely, looking for the trick, and saw they were actually gliding in on boards propelled by the big waves. The riders were not Earthpeople exactly. They reflected the light in an unnatural way and held their limbs a little too rigidly. On the other hand, under the best circumstances I was no expert on Earthpeople. And at the moment, I was a guy who saw things through rainbows.

I watched the boardriders with fascination. Each of them paddled a board out into the ocean to where the water toppled into waves, stood up on the board, and rode in. Sometimes the wave was too much for him, and he toppled too. He'd disappear in the froth for a moment, then bob to the surface; then he and his board would float to the shore, but missing a little dignity.

There were six board-riders, and they repeated this action again and again, as if it were interesting. As if it were fun. I guess it would be if you were doing it instead of watching it. I'd get Whipper Will or one of the others to teach me how.

I don't know how long I stood there watching. Long enough for the rainbows to fade and for me to feel like myself again. The kitchen was solid for the first time. I barely remembered the room where I had awakened.

In another part of the house, something banged. I jumped. Not long after that, Whipper Will came into the room with a stack of thin boxes.

"Make some room on that table, will ya, dude?" he said.

I moved more dishes and pushed aside a metal box that had two wide slits in the top. It was plugged into the wall, but I don't think it was a radio. Whipper Will dropped the boxes with a heavy thunk. "How you doing?"

"Fine, now that the yoyogurt wore off." I watched him carefully. "Though I miss the rainbows."

Whipper Will nodded. "Everybody does. That's why they come back for more."

"There must be a lot of money in yoyogurt." Guys on the radio were always in business for the money. People sometimes died because they wanted too much of it.

"I suppose," said Whipper Will. "But look at this." He held one of the boxes out to me. I took it. On one side was a picture of a guy in a long brown cloth-tube. Something brown perched on his head. Smoke rose from the end of a thin white cylinder that dangled from his mouth. The box opened like a flower, a half circle of sheets bound along one edge. Each sheet was covered with black marks.

"What is it?" I said.

"A library book. Don't you have books where you come from?"

"Not exactly. We have small blocks of wood packed in little cases."

Whipper Will explained the facts of life to me. I heard about fiction, nonfiction, reference books, picture books. All very handy. All very compact.

I said, "All right. I'm impressed. What about these particular books?"

"Raymond Chandler."

"I heard his name on the Philip Marlowe broadcasts."

"Chandler was the hot dog who wrote the original Philip Marlowe stories. I brought these for you to read."

I picked up the book again and flipped through the pages. I stared at the black marks but couldn't force them to make sense. Marlowe was in here somewhere, and I had to find him. *Where you been, Marlowe? I said. He looked more tired than usual. There was a blotch under his eye the size and color of an eggplant. He said, A back room in Bay City. I was knocked as silly as a couple of waltzing mice.*

I said, "I learned to speak English off the radio, remember? I don't know one written word from another."

"Hang loose, will you, bro? That's why I brought these too." He held up a much thinner book. It had colorful pictures and a word or two on each page.

"That looks about right," I said.

Whipper Will and I spent the rest of the day together at what turned out to be the kitchen table. We had baloney sandwiches there at lunchtime. We drank a lot of soda pop. People walked through, sometimes stopped to watch or kibitz, but soon got bored and went about their business.

We had just finished T (T is a Teddy bear Tying his Tennis shoes) and were tired. (T was also for Tired.) After taking a good stretch, Whipper Will asked me if I wanted to see something.

He took me through a tunnel—a hallway—to a small room piled with clothes. It smelled like Earthpeople, only more so.

"My bedroom," he said with pride I did not understand. I stood in the doorway while he clambered over drifts of clothes to a table on which sat the smaller brother of the big eye in the other room.

"This is my computer. You have computers in, uh, Bay City?"

"We get along," I said.

"Sorry," he said, a little embarrassed. "Of course you do. How would you get here, otherwise?"

"Good question," I said. It could mean anything.

"OK. You're from Bay City. Right."

He climbed back into the hall and led me down more tunnels to a small warm room at the back of the house. When he swung open the door, he said, "Sorry about the chlorine smell, but I have to keep this place pretty clean."

I nodded, not understanding. But I could see he'd done a good job. Compared to the rest of the house, where you could break your neck crossing the floor, this room seemed empty. A platoon of shiny glass jars stood on a long counter that divided the room in two. To one side was a refrigerator and a wooden cabinet.

"This is where I make the yoyogurt." He laughed. "Actually *I* don't make it. The bacteria do. I just give them a chance." He took a jar from the wooden cabinet and turned it slowly in front of me. The glop inside was pretty disgusting.

"Pure culture," he said. He saw he was losing his audience and said, "Wanta hear a joke?"

"Sure."

"What's the difference between yogurt and California?"

"I don't know."

"Yogurt has an active culture!"

The joke pleased him. He laughed until I said, "Now I have one. What's the difference between yogurt and yoyogurt?"

"Is that a joke?"

"I don't know. You're the expert."

He meditated on my face for a while, then chuckled deep in his throat. He said, "I'm the only one who knows how to make yoyogurt." He pointed to himself with some pride. "Nothing else has the kick."

He opened a back door and led me outside. Whipper Will had a small fruit-and-vegetable garden back there. "Grow it all myself," he said. "All organic."

"Organic?"

"You know. No pesticides or chemical fertilizers. Wanta see my compost heap?"

I didn't know what a compost heap was, and after he showed it to me, I didn't care. He acted as if he were showing me his private stash of rubies. I nodded and said, "I guess my education is complete now. I've seen a compost heap."

"You haven't even finished the alphabet."

We went back to the kitchen and clawed our way, hand over hand, through the rest of the alphabet. It was a long wait to find out that Z is for Zoot. Punctuation was another matter entirely. The concept was new to me. In Gomkrix you're on your own.

By the time Bingo brought in a pizza for dinner, I could get through one of those kids' ABC books without any trouble.

When the pizza and brewski—otherwise known as beer, I discovered—was gone, Captain Hook and a few of the others took bowls of yoyogurt from the refrigerator. Whipper Will offered me some, but I turned him down. I had work to do that evening, and I'd need my entire brain for it.

Whipper Will left me and joined the rowdy party in the next room. Talk, loud music, and strange smoke filled the air. Occasionally, silence struck suddenly, as if I'd gone deaf, and it seemed even louder than the noise.

While all this was going on, I was reading the top book in the stack, *The Simple Art of Murder* by Raymond Chandler. There were a lot of words in it I didn't know. I made lists and would ask Whipper Will about them later.

But on page twenty I found out why I had come to Earth. There was more to it than just helping Earth-people, and Chandler called the reason by name. He said, "But down these mean streets a man must go who is not himself mean, who is neither tarnished nor afraid. . . . He must be the best man in his world and a good enough man for any world." A good enough man for any world. Rightly or wrongly, I felt that Chandler was talking about me. He had known I was coming. And here I was. Confident of my destiny and of Chandler's blessing, I rested my head on the book and fell asleep.

The next morning was another beautiful day. Most of them are beautiful in Malibu, but I never heard anybody complain. Outside, the board-riders were already at it.

I looked through the kitchen refrigerator and the cabinets for something that might be breakfast. The refrigerator was full of brewski and yoyogurt. I avoided them and pulled out some lonely cold cuts, curled and old. I found some bread in a metal box and built a dry, tasteless sandwich.

I walked outside, and standing in that air was like being wrapped in silk. Still chewing, I walked across the black path, avoiding a very thin woman riding what I guessed was a bicycle. She glanced at me and smiled, but continued on her way.

As I stomped across the warm sand with the wind blowing in my face, the board-riders looked less human, and I became more confused. Oh, they had two arms and two legs apiece, but they reflected the sunlight as if they'd been polished. And though they were graceful, it was the mechanical grace of a machine that was doing its job without thinking or pleasure, not the grace of an animal.

"Oh, wow!" someone cried, despite the fact that I seemed to be alone on the beach.

"Ahh-roooh!" said a voice that was soon joined by others. "Ahh-roooh!"

I came to a place where the beach suddenly fell away as if the ocean had taken a big bite out of it. Below me, all eight of my friends were sitting with their backs against the wall of sand, fiddling with controls on black boxes about the size of a Raymond Chandler novel and howling at the hard blue sky. They were twitching with excitement.

I found my way down to their level, and after watching them stare intensely at the board-riders, I said, "Good morning."

Not one of them looked up at me. They kept working their boxes and watching the water. Whipper Will said, "Hang loose, will you, bro'?"

A moment later, one of the board-riders flipped into the air. He and his board tumbled in opposite directions and fell into the water with splashes I couldn't hear because of the boom of the waves breaking against the shore. "Wipeout!" Whipper Will cried and buried his face in his hands. This had no effect on most of his friends, but Bingo patted his shoulder and said, "Stay cool, bro, Everybody wipes out."

That wasn't what Whipper Will wanted to hear. He shrugged off the girl's hand and stood up. He stalked over to me, and we watched the ocean wash the board and the rider to shore.

While Bingo watched us from one side, I helped Whipper Will drag the rider up onto a sheet of plastic. The board, attached to the rider by a long cord, dragged after. I had a pretty good look at the rider now. It wasn't a person. Not a human or a Toomler or anything else. It was made entirely of brown metal, even to the skimpy bathing suit it wore. Its eyes were empty blue disks.

Whipper Will dropped to his knees and opened a small door in the thing's chest. Inside were enough wires to make a spaghetti dinner and a row of tiny white switches.

I said, "It's cute. What is it?"

Morosely, Whipper Will said, "It's a surf-bot. You know. Like a robot that surfs." He did something with his control box while watching the inside of the surf-bot's chest. The surf-bot jerked its arms and legs.

"It shouldn't have done that. And if I can't figure out why it does that, I'm not even going to *qualify* for the Surf-O-Rama, let alone win."

"Surf-O-Rama?"

"A big surfing contest right here in Malibu. We're sort of the home team."

"I haven't seen you or any of your friends get wet yet."

Whipper Will's eyebrows went up and down as if they'd gone over a bump. He said, "And you won't, either. We don't actually surf ourselves. That's what the robots are for."

"You just control them from the beach."

"Right on. Surf-botting is tougher than it seems. Not just any hodad can do it."

I watched a surf-bot slide as if it were on greased rails along the inside of a wave that was taller than it was. "Anybody *ever* do any real surfing around here?"

"Sure," Whipper Will said, suddenly excited. "Frankie and Annette. They used to make movies back in the sixties. We'll be showing some of them tonight, if you want to see."

"Can't wait," I said.

We stared at the water for a while. The constant rhythmic motion was hypnotic. I was suddenly aware of thunder behind me and realized that it had been going on for a while and was getting louder.

As one, Whipper Will and I turned around. The other surfers came up behind us. We were facing a lot of rolling stock coming our way.

Six of what I guessed to be Earthpeople were riding what were definitely not bicycles, but big black two-wheeled machines with engines that split the early morning silence the way a hammer splits a ripe fruit.

The riders were unlike any Earthpeople I had seen so far. Still, they were enough like Earthpeople that I didn't think they were aliens. Not *very* alien, anyway.

Their skin was cut and blasted, as if they'd spent the night together inside a spinning cement mixer. Their long dirty hair flew out behind them like vines of a plant you would not care to have in the house. Each of them sat far back in his saddle, almost lying down, with his arms stretched to the handlebars, which they handled casually, as if to demonstrate how easy it all was.

They were dressed in black shiny stuff—leather?—and rolled red bandannas wrapped around their heads. I could not see their eyes for the mirrored glasses over them. The riders looked as playful as a slaberingeo's spiked tail.

"Why are we just standing here?" Thumper said.

"Because running wouldn't do any good," Whipper Will said.

"Who are they?" I said.

Without looking at me, Whipper Will said, "Gotterdammerung. They're a motorcycle-punk club that likes to inspire terror in people on the beach."

"Not much of a challenge for them," I said. "Is it a job or a hobby?" Gotterdammerung didn't look any friendlier as it got closer.

They lined up in front of us but did not kill their engines. I did not think it was because they were worried about the need to make a fast getaway.

One of them yelled to us over the sound of the motorcycles, "Yo, surf shit! We got a proposition for ya."

CHAPTER 3
Shut Up and Deal

Gotterdammerung had all the charm of a tragwort, a slaberingeo predator that eats anything if it is hungry enough, which is usually. Gotterdammerung's members could not be ignored, or you would likely lose an arm. *Only* an arm, if you were lucky. Being downwind of them was not a treat.

"What's the haps, Tankhauser?" Whipper Will said. I was impressed at how steady his voice was.

"What is this fuckin' bravado, Will? You wimps are fuckin' scared of us, and you know it."

"You wimps make me sick," another of the choir sang out. This one looked as if, beneath the folds of fat, she might be a female.

"Shut up," Tankhauser explained. Suddenly cozy, he shook his head and said, "Women. I can't get that Goonhilda to close her yap."

Though his statement didn't seem to require an answer, Tankhauser just glared at us for a long time. Maybe he was giving Whipper Will the chance to ask what Gotterdammerung was doing there so he could tell him to shut up. Tankhauser looked like the kind of guy who would never get tired of that kind of fun. Whipper Will didn't say anything.

Gotterdammerung creaked as they shifted in their saddles. Enough chains to haunt a castle crisscrossed their chests and festooned their thick boots. Pictures and writing decorated various parts of their bodies. Eyes on fire and bloody knives seemed popular, as well as ladies in winged helmets. Tankhauser shut off his engine. The others did too. These guys were as good as a chorus line.

It was only a matter of time before Tankhauser noticed me, and now it happened. He said, "Who's the geek with the nose?"

"This is Zoot Marlowe," Whipper Will said. "Zoot, this is Tankhauser and his friends, Goonhilda, Sickfred, Dollkyrie, Wortan and Thor-head." Not one of them moved. I did not rate so much as a nod.

Tankhauser said, "You'll let anybody onto this beach, won't you?"

I wanted to say, "Obviously," but for my health I let it pass.

Whipper Will said, "You're right, Tank. Not much of a beach. What brings you here? You can't be out of yoyogurt already."

"I can if I want, but I'm not," Tankhauser said with the petulance of a small child. "What I'm out of is patience." He kind of flexed his hands. "I don't like comin' down here and giving you surf shit money for yoyogurt. I wanna make it myself."

"It's not as easy as you think."

"Don't give me that crap. A little sour milk."

The waves pummeled the shore. The sun beat down. Gulls bobbed and weaved overhead. All very

pleasant if you weren't waiting for some yabo to pull
out his knife and do a little informal surgery.

Whipper Will said, "We don't charge you half what
we could."

"Wimps," Wortan grumbled. He had a thick curly
beard and collected his hair up under a flat leather
hat. If anything, he did not seem as bright as Tankhauser.

Tankhauser looked cagey—an eye-squinting gri-
mace that hung on his face as naturally as an extra
lip—and spoke with all the sincerity of a salesman
with his fingers crossed. He said, "Maybe you do and
maybe you don't. We ain't barbarians."

"We know that, Tank—"

"Shut up. We ain't barbarians, so we ain't gonna
just chain-whip you till you tell us what we want to
know."

As grateful as he was for this, Tankhauser's kind-
ness surprised Whipper Will. "What will you do,
Tank?"

"We challenge you to a duel."

"I'm not much with a chain, Tank."

"Right. But you guys are hell on surfboards."

Tankhauser let that sink in. I didn't understand
what was going on. Why *didn't* Gotterdammerung just
take what they wanted? Unless I read human psy-
chology all wrong, it didn't make sense.

"Right on," said Whipper Will as he nodded. I felt
better now that he seemed to be as confused as I was.
"Surfboards at twenty paces."

Tankhauser began to heat up; I could see the pres-
sure building. But the redness went back to hide behind his ears, and he only said, "Twerp, you take a
lotta chances. Listen: The big Surf-O-Rama is coming

up. If we win, you give us the yoyogurt recipe. If you win—" Gotterdammerung laughed. Deranged monkey laughter. It was not a pretty thing to hear. "If you win, we leave the beach forever."

"You guys don't know anything about surf-bots."

"That's our problem," Tankhauser said. He smiled. His face did not crack, but it was a near thing.

Whipper Will went into a huddle with the other surfers. I was not invited. That meant I was left with nothing to look at but Gotterdammerung, and they had nothing to look at but me.

"Hey," said Thor-head, "where'd you get that beak, Marlowe?"

"Shaddup," Tankhauser said. He cleaned his nails with the big knife he took from his belt. I don't think that *clean* was a concept that came easy to him, but he must have enjoyed imagining he might cut himself. The other members of Gotterdammerung watched the ocean. I shifted from one foot to the other.

"Try not to do anything stupid," Tankhauser said without looking up.

A moment later, the surfers broke from their huddle, and Whipper Will said, "OK, Tank. Chew-on-it? Chew-got-it."

"OK. We ain't talking about anybody else. Just surfer total points against Gotterdammerung total points."

"Right," Whipper Will said.

With the sound of a giant clearing his throat, Tankhauser started his engine. The others followed suit. Not far away, a crowd of gulls that had been waiting on the sand leaped into the air and circled, cawing how displeased they were at the noise.

Without another word, Gotterdammerung turned

and roared back across the sand. A few minutes later they were gone. Except for the tire tracks and the metallic taste at the back of my mouth, they might never have been there.

"Pretty aggro," Thumper said.

Whipper Will said, "What do you think, Zoot?"

I said, "Me? If I think about those guys, I get a headache. Any of them know how to use a surf-bot?"

Captain Hook said, "Those guys know three things: motorcycles, fighting, and yoyogurt."

"Four things," Whipper Will said. He and his friends chuckled wryly.

"I assume the fourth thing is not surf-botting," I said. "If that's true, then I think our wallets have just been lifted, and we don't know it yet."

While the rest of them surfed—what passed for surfing in a world too full of technology—I asked Whipper Will the questions that I had written down the night before. I could read pretty well, and though the grammar had more twists than a corkscrew, I could manage that too. But I needed to have an entire world of words explained. Whipper Will was pretty good at it. Using a dictionary and a lot of talk, we did all right.

At one point I said, "What's your story, Will?"

"Story?"

"Sure. There must be one. You're not like the others."

"What do you mean?"

"Those others could sit on the beach all day and let their brains fry. They don't have any more idea how to make yoyogurt than Gotterdammerung, and it doesn't bother them. They're nice folks, understand, just not interested in the finer things. You, on the other hand, seem to have a knack for teaching and the academic. Otherwise I'd be sitting here alone."

Whipper Will looked at the table and idly flicked the pages of *Farewell, My Lovely* with a thumb. He said, "I used to teach professionally." He didn't say any more for a while.

"Is that it?" I said.

"Might as well be."

"Fair enough."

One way and another, it was an illuminating afternoon. After dinner we gathered in the living room for what they called some classic flicks.

The living room was the room I'd awakened in that first morning. The stuff in it wasn't just stuff now. It all had names. The rattling white sheets were newspapers. The books of slick colored pictures were magazines. Seashells hung from fishnet draped artistically across one wall. In a corner, incense smoked next to a churning Lava Lite. Old beer cans and yoyogurt dishes peppered a jumble of big dirty pillows.

Yammering and laughing, the surfers scattered around the room. The system seemed to be for the girls to sit cross-legged on the floor with the guys stretched out before them, their heads in the girls' laps. The girls played with the boys' hair. The boys didn't seem to mind. These weren't the mating rituals I was used to on T'toom, but they weren't so different, either. The point of young love is always the same. Mustard began to build funny little cigarettes from thin papers and dry leaves. People took them eagerly, lit them up, and inhaled mightily.

Bingo passed one of the cigarettes to me. I took it and inhaled as I had seen the others do. The food hadn't killed me. A little smoke should be safe enough. The sweet-tasting smoke went through my brain as if it were a sieve. Every muscle in my body relaxed. Far away, I think cow bells tinkled. I tried to inhale again, but Bingo took the cigarette away from me. She said, "Go easy. You don't want to get lost inside your own head."

"No. There are places there I'd rather not visit."

Bingo handed the cigarette to Whipper Will, who took a puff and crawled on his hands and knees to the big eye in a box, the television. Too bad we hadn't received television broadcasts on T'toom. But then all those artists with their artists' conceptions of humans would have been out of work.

Whipper Will sorted through some rectangular boxes, slid a black plastic box from its cardboard sleeve, and shoved it into a slot in the front of the television. He turned around and sat down hard on the floor, his arms resting on his knees. He said, "Guys and gals, dudes and chicks, geeks and freaks, you'll be really stoked about the flick we have tonight."

Captain Hook and Thumper cried, "Ahh-roooh!" while everybody but Mustard applauded. Mustard was leaning back in Flopsie's lap—or was it Mopsie's?—and staring at the ceiling through a cloud of smoke he'd just blown from his mouth.

When the outburst wound down into quiet laughter, Whipper Will said, "Tonight, Gino and Darlene in *Beach Bunny Bash.*"

"What remainder bin did you find *that* in?" Captain Hook called out. His question got a laugh. Which was probably the idea.

"Get stuffed," Whipper Will said in a friendly tone.

"It won't hurt you hodads to watch something besides *Beach Blanket Bingo* for a change."

"We ain't got Annette's tits memorized yet," Thumper said and laughed loudly. Captain Hook punched him in the shoulder.

"If you dudes are done with the floor show," Whipper Will said and pushed a button on the television. The eye came alive with colored confetti. Music began, heavy on some string instrument and a drum. The words "Beach Bunny Bash" splashed across the screen.

Whether it was a good movie, I didn't know, never having seen a movie before. But it was interesting to somebody who knew as little as I did about Earthpeople and their culture. Or cultures. I gathered from the plot that not everybody agreed on the best way to get along.

As we watched, Whipper Will or Bingo would lean over and whisper an explanation to me. The rest of the surfers were too busy smoking and joking to be much help, or even to watch the movie very closely.

"Why do you show these things if nobody pays attention?" I said.

Whipper Will said, "The people who made these movies used a standard formula on purpose. They assumed that there would be more action in the audience than on the screen."

"Action?"

"Don't you people have sex where you come from?" Bingo said. The thought of a world without sex evidently offended her.

"Sure. But we don't have the movies to go along with it."

"Right," Whipper Will went on. "So the plot kind

of cruises along. Anybody who's seen one or two beach movies could come in halfway through and have a good chance of knowing what was going on."

"Sounds about as exciting as watching the clothes go around in a washing machine."

"Tradition."

I could have said something nifty and crude to that, but there was no point insulting my host for no good reason. I watched the movie instead. It was about Gino and Darlene.

He was a poor but honest surfer-boy who hung out on the beach and took odd jobs to pay the bills. She was a rich girl with a taste for excitement. They were just a couple of kids who were ripe for, well, being ripe. At first, Gino thought Darlene was a snob, and Darlene thought Gino was a slob. Then Darlene went out surfing by herself after only one lesson. Gino saved her life. They fell in love while she was getting dry next to a fire Gino had built on the beach.

Well, it went on. When nothing much was happening music swelled—that's the word—out of nowhere. It was usually a song about true love or the perfect wave, or both at once. Motorcycle maniacs much like Gotterdammerung confused the situation. Eventually the surfers succeeded in getting the motorcycle maniacs kicked off the beach permanently. Gino and Darlene decided to finish high school before they got married. The end.

"Do humans watch this kind of stuff all the time?"

"Well," said Whipper Will, "sometimes there's Shakespeare."

"Oh yeah? Who wrote it?"

Whipper Will just nodded. He said, "When you fin-

ish the Chandler, I'll give you the complete plays. It'll
cure you of your ignorance or kill you."

By this time most of the couples in the room were
either asleep or so involved with themselves that they
might as well have been alone. Whipper Will and
Bingo and I sat up and talked for a while. Then they
went off to Whipper Will's room and I went to the
kitchen to read some more Chandler. The kitchen was
too bright after the companionable dimness of the living room. I got engrossed in *The Big Sleep*. It wasn't
Shakespeare, but according to Whipper Will nothing
but Shakespeare ever is.

I awoke at the kitchen table the next morning. This
was getting to be a habit I'd like to break. I stood,
stretching the kinks out of my muscles while I looked
out the window. Nobody was out there surfing, not
even machinery.

Nobody was in the living room. I walked along the
hallway to the back of the house, listening to shouts
and angry conversation get louder. I could not yet understand what was being said, but the tone was un-
mistakable.

I went out the back door and walked along the path
through the vegetable garden to a smaller white building not connected to the house. Maybe this was a garage. The loud talk was coming from there. Nobody
invited me. The door was open, so I just walked in.

Inside the garage, Captain Hook was marching up
and down before a circle of his friends, waving his
hands in the air. His friends were in shock. Everything about them slumped. They had their hands
stuffed deep in their pockets and their empty eyes
were deep in their heads. Captain Hook was talking,

but what he said wasn't the problem. It wasn't even interesting to them. "I don't know, dude," Captain Hook said. "We can't just stand around hanging loose."

"All right, hot dog," Whipper Will said. "*You* be the kahuna. I'm tired." He rubbed his face with both hands as if trying to rearrange his features.

"Is this a private party?" I said.

"Come on in, dude," Whipper Will said.

Captain Hook spun on me and said, "Talk about hot dogs. A hodad hot dog." He growled as Whipper Will showed me a line of surf-bots laying on the cement as if they were asleep. Every one was badly dented or had a limb torn off, showing untidy clumps of wires.

"You ought to take better care of your equipment," I said.

Captain Hook laughed, sounding as if he were choking.

Whipper Will said, "Looks as if somebody got stoked on sledgehammers, doesn't it?"

I smiled and said, "Looks like a mystery to me."

CHAPTER 4
Good Enough For Any World

So, I hadn't come to Earth for nothing. Here I was at the scene of an actual crime. I'd solve it because it was the right thing to do, because somebody had to do justice. That's why I was on Earth. Not to help the Earthpeople, but to do justice. Me and Marlowe. Marlowe and me.

Captain Hook said something under his breath.

"What?" I said.

"I said, 'Gotterdammerung.' "

"Evidence?" I said.

"Who else would do this?" Captain Hook said.

"I like my evidence a little warmer than that."

Captain Hook was on me in two strides, and intending to do to me what somebody had done to the surf-bots. I socked him hard in the chest. A small *oof* of air escaped from his mouth, and he fell backward onto the floor, having no more idea what hit him than a puppy. The noise he made was strangely satisfying, reminding me of the fights I'd heard on the radio. Obviously, I'd hit him right. I waited for him to come at me again, but his anger had burned out. He rubbed his chest and smiled up at me in a sleepy way.

"Pretty aggro, dude. I'll bet Tankhauser and you would rip pretty good."

"I'd rather live," I said. I looked at Whipper Will and said, "What about Gotterdammerung?"

"They're a boss bet, all right, but nobody knows their hang."

"Hang?" I said.

"Hangout. Home is where they park their motorcycles."

"Somebody must know," Bingo said.

"What do we do when we find them? Spank them?"

"OK," said Captain Hook. "You be the kahuna. You tell us what to do."

"Let me think," I said and walked out of the garage. I mooned around the garden for a while. It was cool, smelled good, and reminded me of the forests of home. I searched the roses and carrots and tomatoes for ideas. Flopsie and Mopsie pretended to be weeding, but they spent more time watching me than concentrating on their work.

After a while, Whipper Will came out of the house looking thoughtful. He joined me next to some pink explosions of flowers and said, "We've been calling around to the usual places where we buy parts for our surf-bots."

"Yes?"

He was having difficulty choosing the right words, as if talk was not cheap. "Nobody has anything."

"What does that mean?"

"Just what I said. There are no surf-bot parts of any description to be had, not even for ready money. Nothing. Zip. Zilch. Not so much as a coil of wire."

"Anybody say why not?"

"It's all been sold."

"To whom?"

"Nobody would say. Maybe they didn't know."

"How could that be?"

"This is a big deal. They may have a name on an invoice or a bill of sale, but my guess is that that name would be a dead, end. The rich dudes really behind this will know how to keep their business to themselves."

"Does Gotterdammerung have that kind of money?"

"No way, Ho-zay. Sometimes they have trouble coming up with enough to pay for the yoyogurt they want. Of course, they'd be easy to hire."

"That leaves us with the question of *who* has hired them. So much for Captain Hook's terrific theory. Let's try something else."

We went into the house together. From the looks of the occupants, somebody had just died.

Thumper and Mustard were on the couch. Hanger was sitting on the floor between Mustard's knees. They were looking in the direction of the television, but their faces were as empty as the space between stars. The people on television, who at the moment were jumping up and down in front of a new automobile, could have saved themselves the trouble.

In the kitchen, Captain Hook sat at the table, his leg bouncing by itself. He was concentrating on a figure-eight he made over and over again in the condensation on the side of a beer can. He took a long drink, and put the can down as if he had not done anything.

He looked up when we came into the kitchen, and kind of lolled back in his straight-backed wooden chair. Lolling was not easy to do in that chair. He'd had practice. He said, "Hot on the case, are we, sha-mus?"

"Hot enough to know that Gotterdammerung ei-ther had nothing to do with this or was hired by a big boy we'll have a lot of trouble finding."

Captain Hook shook his head and twisted a beer out of its plastic carrier. "Have a brewski. Have enough of them, it won't matter anymore."

"I like your style, Captain Hook. You always have a solution."

He set the can on the table carefully, as if the can and the table were made of glass. Tears glistened in his eyes, and I realized that he and the others were just kids. They were really ripped about losing their surf-bots—not just because the 'bots were expensive doodads, but because the Surf-O-Rama was coming up. Without surf-bots, the kids couldn't defend their honor.

Whipper Will wasn't a kid. He was old enough to be the father of any of the others, and I liked him, but that wasn't enough to know. Not by half. He squeezed Captain Hook's shoulder and said, "Get mellow, dude. Zoot's on the case."

Captain Hook nodded, but without enthusiasm.

Will showed me how to use the telephone and the telephone book. I picked a new robot dealer at ran-dom and punched in the number.

"Endless Summer."

"Hey, bro'," I said. "I'd like to buy a surf-bot."

"Sorry. We don't have any."

"This *is* a surf-bot store, isn't it?"

"For sure. We just don't have any right now."

"When do you expect more?" I tried to keep my

voice pleasant, but a certain sarcastic note must have crept in.

The Endless Summer clerk said, "Wait a minute," and I heard muffled voices. A moment later, a gruff voice came on the line and said, "I don't know when we'll get more surf-bots. Try The Happy Hot Dog over on Camino del Oro."

"They told me to try you," I ad-libbed.

The gruff voice was silent for a moment, as if I'd surprised him. He said, "Sorry," and hung up.

I set the phone into its cradle and stood there with my hand on it. I said nothing, having nothing to say.

"Well?" Captain Hook said. There was light behind his eyes again.

I said, "Somebody's buying up all the *new* robots in town too."

"Which means?" There was a nasty, impatient tone in his voice.

"Lighten up, Captain," Whipper Will said.

I said, "It means nuts. I might as well have a brewski. The smart stuff isn't getting me anywhere." I didn't move.

Whipper Will said, "Why get ripped about any of this? It isn't your problem."

"I'm staying in your house. Eating your food. I owe you something."

"Wash the dishes. It's not so hard on the brain."

"Yuck," I said. Whipper Will and Captain Hook laughed. But not very hard, and not very long.

Whipper Will said, "You were already stoked about detective work when you showed up. Why?"

I sighed and said, "I didn't know myself till I read the essay in *The Simple Art of Murder*."

"Mean streets?"

"You got it. Also, I figure that I'm a good enough man for any world." Whipper Will didn't remember that part of the quote, and I had to repeat it to him.

"What is that?" Captain Hook said. "Code?"

"It's in the book," Whipper Will said. "Right there on top of the stack."

Captain Hook picked up *The Simple Art of Murder* and held it as if it were a bomb. He turned a couple of pages and shrugged. "I can't concentrate. Too cranked on beer, I guess." He looked at me. "*Get* those aggro dudes," he said, and walked outside to stare at the ocean. It kept rolling in, no matter what.

Whipper Will said, "I guess we know where each other's heads are at."

"You might know where my head is at. About you I still have nothing but questions."

That seemed to please him. Through his smile he said, "What's next?"

I said, "I'll need a few things."

"Like what?"

"I know all the words. Fedora. Trench coat. Chrysler."

"All simple enough except maybe that last. What about a gun?"

"I've never fired one, but I ought to have one anyway, I guess. If only for appearance's sake."

Whipper Will grinned and said, "In the private eye biz, appearances are everything."

I grinned back at him. We were just a couple of cool private eye experts.

He went into his bedroom for a moment and emerged wearing a pair of faded cloth shoes. They had probably once been blue. He was folding some green paper into the pocket of his jeans.

"Is that money?" I said.

"That's it." He handed me a sheet and I studied it.

I said, "It doesn't look like the kind of thing that would cause so much trouble." I handed it back.

"You'll see," he said and led me out the front door.

The front of the house was stucco with fake half-timbering painted a powerful blue. There were no windows on this side, and no sidewalk, just a three-car parking lot, currently empty. Heavy traffic boomed by on a wide street. It sounded like the ocean, but had no predictable rhythm. The sound just went on and on, never stopping for breath. I'd never seen anything like it, and I hung back from it. "Mean streets" took on a whole new meaning.

"Pacific Coast Highway," Whipper Will said. "It's the seam that sews the edge of the continent to the Pacific Ocean. Known to its friends as PCH."

"We can be friends if it wears a muzzle."

Whipper Will pulled me along the edge of PCH to a crosswalk that had a traffic light at each end. I had seen this stuff on television, but I hadn't quite believed it. Seeing it in person was a shock.

People of all ages, colors, and types stared at me as they walked past. A guy and a gal, a matched blond set suitable to be used as bookends, giggled after they'd passed, but nobody said a word to me. They just carried their surfboards, 'bots, or baskets full of food.

The light changed to green in our direction, and we strolled across the street. Considering all I'd heard about how dangerous Earthpeople were, I was amazed that a red light would really stop all that traffic. But it did, and we crossed to the other side of the street safely.

The far side of PCH was crowded with little shops huddled together around postage-stamp parking lots. We passed a couple of rent-a-'bot stores, but they looked sad with their empty windows and Closed signs. Whoever had bought up surf-bots had been thorough.

I had plenty of opportunities to buy T-shirts or pizza, though. Whipper Will walked past the stores as if they weren't there. He stopped for a moment to study a window full of surfboards, clucked over the prices, and went on till we came to a shopping mall.

I suppose it was not a big place as shopping malls go—barely large enough to use as an airfield. But it was full of noise and color and strange smells, anything the owners could think of to pull in the suckers. I stood just inside the door looking at the levels above us. The ceiling disappeared in a cloud of colorful plastic balloons that hung from poles. The place was crowded with people who were full of purpose—like bloodhounds on the scent.

I caused less commotion than I thought I would. People who noticed me at all looked away immediately. Maybe they really thought I had a birth defect and didn't want to seem impolite. Still, nobody likes to feel like a geek. I found myself wanting somebody to take a good look at me just once. It never happened.

Whipper Will grabbed me by the arm and pulled me across the tile floor to a place called For Men Only.

"Cute," I said.

"That's the stock-in-trade around here," he said.

Inside was rack after rack of clothes like the ones the men in the newspaper photographs wore—long cloth tubes in muted colors. "I guess the name of the store doesn't mean much," I said, nodding in the direction of one of the many women pawing through the merchandise.

"Not much," Whipper Will agreed.

A fat man with a small mustache and worried eyes hurried up to us. He nodded in my direction but spoke to Whipper Will. Maybe he thought I was Will's pet.

Will told him what I needed. The salesman wet his lips and ran them under his teeth while he pulled a threadbare tape measure from a pocket. He measured me quickly and sighed when he backed off. "This way, please."

We followed the salesman across the big room to a rack of suits under a sign that said Young Men and Boys. He rummaged along the rack until he found what he was looking for. It was a brown suit and it fit pretty well considering it was made for an Earthman.

Whipper Will used his cash to buy it and a long brown coat and a fedora. When I had them all on at once, I looked like the guy on the cover of *The Simple Art of Murder*—except for my nose, which was still several sizes too big for a human's, and a cigarette, which I did not have. But I looked like a detective now. If looking like a detective was all it took to be a detective, I'd be all right.

CHAPTER 5
Fake Detective

I wanted to buy some shoes to go with my outfit. Gum shoes. Whipper Will smiled when I said that, but he didn't object. In the mall's shoe store, Step On It, the salesman morosely studied my feet while he rubbed his chin and grunted.

"Sandals?" he said hopefully.

"Gum shoes."

"Hmm." He crossed the shoe store and talked to a big guy who had spent all the time since Whipper Will and I had come in drumming his fingers on the cash register. The two fat salesmen watched me while they gestured to each other and spoke in guttural whispers. At last they came to a decision.

Looking as proud as if he'd just figured out how to charge people for using gravity, the guy marched back and told me that what I needed was an orthopedic shoe store.

"What does that mean?"

He glanced back at his friend and, suddenly looking as uncomfortable as a worm at a bird convention, said, "Well, you have unusual feet."

"Unusual," Whipper Will said without expression.

The salesman glanced at him, tried on a smile, but it didn't fit and it slid off.

"Is there an orthopedic shoe store in the mall?" I said.

"No." Having a ready answer seemed to relieve him. He was back on top of things again.

Whipper Will and I walked back to the house. The new jacket and shirt were tight under my arms, but the pants were a little loose despite how far over I had pulled the belt. I found a pair of shoes at last—the largest pair they'd had in a sporting goods store. The salesman had continued to shake his head even as he took Whipper Will's money.

I probably didn't look any stranger than I had in the clothing I had arrived in. And I was considerably less strange than some of the people we passed walking along PCH. I swaggered a little as I walked, caught myself, and tried to slouch as I imagined Philip Marlowe might, tired after a long, fruitless day of investigating.

"What will you do with that stuff?" Whipper Will said as he tapped the brown paper bundle I carried under one arm.

"Keep it. When I go back to, er, Bay City, I'll need my old clothes."

"You're going back?"

"I didn't come all this way not to go back."

"I guess that makes sense."

"It's deep. Deeper than the deep blue sea."

Whipper Will got me safely across Pacific Coast Highway again, and he jingled some keys to let us into the house. Things had livened up a little since we'd gone. Everybody was in the living room sitting in front of the television, engrossed in some kind of moving drawing of a muscular guy destroying a building with light that shot from his fingers. I watched for a few minutes and decided I'd rather spend time inside a bass drum than keep watching.

After a while, Captain Hook noticed us. He stood up and turned off the television. No one protested. They were all looking at me and my new clothes. "Who paid for the threads?" Thumper said, as if he already knew an answer he did not like.

"We did," said Captain Hook.

Whipper Will nodded.

I said, "Think of it as a retainer."

"You can find the dudes who trashed our stuff?"

"I can look. I'll find them if they're findable."

The room was silent. Across the sand, the ocean whispered secrets to the shore.

"No guarantees, huh?"

"Not a one. I can't read the future any better than you can. I can only try my best."

"Shit," Captain Hook said and turned on the television again. Seconds later, the room was full of loud music and the spectacle of this drawing of a muscular guy throwing a drawing of a rock that was bigger than he was. Evidently, the discussion was over.

Whipper Will took me into his bedroom and shut the door. The smell in the room reminded me again how different humans and Toomlers really were. He opened a drawer and from under a pile of fruit-colored clothes, he took something that he held up for me. It was long and black and had a handle. Beyond that, it had no more meaning than what I'd seen on the television.

"What is it?"

"It's a pistol." He handed it to me. It seemed very

light and not very sturdy. On the side it said, "OK SILL NOVELTY COMPANY, HONG KONG in raised letters. "If this thing shoots bullets then I'm Orson Welles."

"It doesn't shoot bullets. It shoots water."

"A water pistol? Who's that supposed to scare, the petunias?"

"Ever fired a real gun?"

"Well, no."

"Then you're safer with this one. Besides, it looks like a real pistol and it *does* shoot water. That could buy you a little time if you ever need it."

I hefted the water pistol. It might be better than nothing at all, but just barely. It wouldn't make me cocky. That was a good thing, anyway. I said, "Why do you keep it hidden?"

"It's mine. I've had it since I was a kid. I don't want anybody borrowing it. Things get broken."

"*I* might break it."

"You might. But you're a gnarly guy, and you might not. Besides, it's for a good cause."

He took me into the bathroom and showed me how to fill the pistol with water. When it was full it felt more substantial, as if it might be worth something in a pinch.

Whipper Will went off to make a batch of yoyogurt while I walked into the backyard and had some target practice. After a while, Whipper Will came out to watch. I fired at a white, velvety blossom that had never hurt anybody. It bent back when the spurt of water hit it, then swayed, throwing around droplets. Whipper Will said, "You're a cool dude, Zoot."

"Sure. Fastest drip in the west. If flowers are behind this mess, we're all set."

A salty wind blew through the garden, making the plants wave at me. I hoped they weren't waving bye-bye. I took a snootful of the crisp 'Bu air and, big as my snoot was, there was still some left over. Whipper Will knelt, pulled a weed, and rolled it into a ball between his hands. He put the weed into his pocket.

I said, "There's just one more thing."

He looked at me as if waiting for me to hatch.

"I'll need a car."

"Right on." He walked across the yard. Having nothing better to do, I followed him. He led me into the garage and walked around the line of sorry surf-bots. They were still lying on the cement floor, cold and lonely. I don't think anybody had touched them since they'd been discovered. Beyond the 'bots, Whipper Will pulled a big sheet off a form I hadn't noticed before back in a dim corner of the garage. Under the sheet was an automobile.

It was long and white, and it had fins. Someone had polished it recently. It was the most beautiful thing I'd ever seen.

To my unanswered question, Whipper Will said, "A 1960 Chevrolet Belvedere. In more or less mint condition."

"I was hoping for a Chrysler, like Marlowe drives."

"Would you know a Chrysler if you saw one?"

"No."

"Then you might as well drive this."

"Terrific. Fake gun. Fake car."

"For a fake detective."

"Yeah. Who's going to drive it?"

He'd been blowing away dust motes that may or may not have been there. Now he looked over at me and said, "Cowabunga! I forgot. Get in."

Drive the car? Durf, I didn't even know how to open the door.

Whipper Will opened the garage door, then got into the car next to me. He was behind the wheel. We sat with our backs to Pacific Coast Highway, still snarling as traffic rushed past. The sun was high and the world was bright.

I put the water pistol into the glove compartment and, with a flourish, Whipper Will took keys from a pocket, inserted them into a slot on the dashboard—so that's what a dashboard was!—and started the engine. It growled like a healthy lion, then settled down and hummed.

He looked over his shoulder as he carefully backed out. He let a red light stop traffic for him, and he backed into the street so fast, we bounced. A moment later I was trying to keep from clawing my way into the back seat. The Chevrolet Belvedere zipped right along, not slowing much as it swooped into spaces in front of slower cars.

"Chill out," Whipper Will said. Nothing bothered him. He had one hand on the wheel, and the other rested on the window ledge. Iron Man Will.

"I've never gone this fast."

"No? Bay City's a lot closer than I thought."

"Yeah. Never this fast this close to the ground."

"If you're going to live on Earth, you'd better get used to it."

We drove for what seemed like hours. Eventually, I calmed down enough to notice what kind of country we were moving through. On one side was the beach and then the ocean. On the other side were cliffs that rose higher than I could see out the front window of the car. Sometimes they were just bare cliffs, worn by wind and water into long artistic furrows. At their feet, between scrub brush and broken glass, were shopping malls and little shops selling fried chicken and pizza. There were surf-bot stores too, but they didn't seem to be doing much business.

Whipper Will made a left turn—a beautiful maneuver that I did not yet care to try—and drove inland along a twisting highway with one lane in either direction. He pulled onto a narrow road among the hills and came at last to a big sign that said, IGNAZIO'S FINE ITALIAN FOOD.

Beyond the sign, which itself was not in good shape, was a building that no one had thought much about for a long time. It was a dump covered with peeling paint that might have once been a gaudy red. Twisted, half-dead plants stood along the wall like old soldiers who needed their pensions. Every window I could see was either broken or boarded up. But between the sign and the dump was an empty parking lot.

Whipper Will stopped the car in the middle of the cracked asphalt of the lot. We sat for a moment listening to birds tell each other all about it. The air was full of spicy smells. They came from the hills around us, not from the dead restaurant. Then Will said, "OK. Your turn." He came around to my side and got in. He pushed me over until I was under the wheel.

I wasn't as tall as he was by a long shot, but I managed to reach the pedals and look out the windshield at the same time. When I started the engine, it squealed as if I'd stepped on its toe.

"You gotta let go of the starter after it starts the car."

I glared at Whipper Will but tried again. This time, the engine started smoothly, as it had for him. I put the car into gear. The car leaned forward, but I had my foot on the brake and we didn't go anywhere. I took my foot off the brake, and I was driving.

The wheel seemed to have a mind of its own, but I wrestled with it and didn't quite hit a suicidal tree that stepped in front of the car.

"It's easier to drive a spaceship," I said. "Computers do most of the work for you."

"Sissy stuff," Whipper Will said.

I just grunted.

Whipper Will spent most of the afternoon teaching me to drive. It wasn't really hard to do once you figured out how to make your feet and your hands do six different things all at once. I drove in big circles and in figure-eights. I backed into imaginary parking spaces, in the process not destroying more than a small fleet of imaginary parked cars. After a while, it was even fun.

When our little valley of automotive excellence was in shadow, and just the tops of the hills caught the gold of the setting sun, Whipper Will asked the big question. He asked me if I wanted to drive us back to the house. I didn't, but I said I did.

"You seem very relaxed about all this," I said.

"I'm a very cool dude. Besides, appearances can be deceiving. Move 'em out."

The two-lane road was nearly empty, but the traffic got heavier as we approached PCH, which was as crowded as a bag of marbles.

"Room for one more?" I said.

"Impossible traffic is a California tradition," Whipper Will said.

I managed to get between a semitrailer and a small car without a top. The small car was driven by a guy wearing a suit and sunglasses. The guy, thinking that somehow I could go faster, maybe right over the top of the semi, honked at me. I thought of the water pistol in the glove compartment.

Eventually, the guy in the little car swung around me and actually got about a half a car-length ahead of me before I made a very snappy left turn into the garage at the surfers' house. I turned off the engine and sat there breathing hard.

Whipper Will said, "Not bad."

I nodded and said, "I heard something once about needing a license to operate one of these things. All those people out there have licenses?"

"Probably not," Whipper Will said. "You don't need a license to drive—just to get caught."

I nodded and said, "You're talking to the invisible man."

CHAPTER 6
Tough Patter

It was a wild night. After all the disappointments of the day, after the cartoon shows and the brewskis, my friends went a little crazy. They played loud music and they danced with wide, sinuous motions. They passed around the funny cigarettes and ate strawberry yoyogurt. The television was on too, but with the sound turned down. It showed tense conversations and car chases and shootouts and happy couples taking the right medicine, all in mysterious silence. No one in the room paid any of this the least attention. The television was just a flickering light source, throwing unsubstantial shadows through the cloud of odd smoke at the wall, where they moved with the dancers and, to my surprise, stuck just like regular shadows.

But the party was a little too hysterical, as if my friends were trying to forget the surf-bot corpses out in the garage, as if they were proving they could have a good time despite everything.

Mostly, I sat in a corner of the room watching these unfamiliar tribal dances of natives from another planet. I swayed a little with the music. After all, I'd had a yoyogurt or two myself, and I'd been breathing that funny cloud for hours with that big devil of a nose of mine. I was strolling around inside myself, but so far the neighborhood was familiar. I was not lost yet.

Giggling, Flopsie and Mopsie came over to my corner and one of them sat on either side of me. I wondered if they were considered good-looking. I supposed they were. None of the surfer guys had any trouble dancing very close to them and taking liberties with their bodies. The girls began to cuddle with me. It was all very playful, like a couple of kids playing tickle-bee with their favorite uncle. I considered telling them to stop. There was a lot to consider. Meanwhile, nobody told Flopsie and Mopsie to stop.

It was fun, and I kind of lost track of the time, and the next thing I knew, Flopsie and Mopsie were sitting back on their heels giggling and pointing at the place between my legs. I looked down and saw that my pants were around my ankles. I wanted to say something to them, something cute and biting, just like Marlowe, but my brain seemed to be sitting inside somebody else's body. I meant to say, "What's so funny?" but I only grunted.

Flopsie or Mopsie called her friends over. Only Bingo was still dancing. Whipper Will was eyeball to eyeball with the television—watching the colored dots jump. The rest of the folks were gone. In pairs, I supposed. Bingo came over to take a look at me. "Cowabunga," she exhaled. "Is that how they hang in Bay City?"

"Hang what?" I said. Somebody said, using my mouth. I felt myself falling sideways but was asleep before I hit the floor.

* * *

I knew I had been asleep because the next morning I woke up. I was in the same corner I'd been the night before. I was the only person in the room, though the remains of last night's party still littered the floor. I don't know if I'd moved in the night, but every muscle in my body ached. I sat there for a while twitching lethargically and enjoying it, wondering what I would do that day. I remembered with a shock: Today I was a detective, and I had a case.

The kitchen was full of the kind of sunlight they talk about in travel brochures. Through the big window, I could see my friends throwing a sneeve around on the beach. Whipper Will had told me that the sneeve was called a Frisbee, and that it was made of plastic. A lot of things on Earth were made of plastic. I guess humans couldn't smell the flat, dank odor it gave off.

I had some toast with jelly and a couple of cups of coffee. It is our loss that we have no coffee on T'toom. If we could import coffee along with that Malibu sunlight, I could pay Dad back for the secondhand sneeve in which I'd flown to Earth a lot quicker than either of us had thought.

While I ate, I leafed through the telephone book looking for companies that made surf-bots and surf-bot parts. If I could talk to the people who made the stuff, find out why they were not stocking the stores, it might bring me one step closer to whoever was behind the buy-up and the sledgehammer job. It might. No promises. Never any promises.

The first name on the list was the Acme Robot Company at an address in Culver City. I consulted the Thomas Bros. map book Whipper Will had left out for me and found that the address wasn't too far away. Not for a guy who'd already come all the way from T'toom.

I wrote a note for Whipper Will telling him where I was going and left it on the refrigerator behind a magnet in the shape of a surfboard.

The Belvedere was where I'd left it the previous afternoon, but not quite so shiny as it had been before I drove it. I opened the garage door and got behind the wheel and started the engine like some working-class hero going to work. And then I noticed the white envelope on the dash. It had my name on it. Inside was one hundred bucks in cash and a note from Whipper Will telling me not to spend it all in one place. Was it bad luck on Earth to spend all your money in one place, or just a bad idea? I folded the money into my pants pocket.

Using the red light on PCH as a barricade, I backed into the street and drove to Culver City.

Traffic was light, and I sailed up PCH, not caring to take the chances that Whipper Will took when he drove. It was a heady experience driving by myself, and I got to feeling as if the world were no more than that mottled blue ball I had seen from space, and I had it in my trench coat pocket.

I drove up the incline at Colorado Boulevard and into Santa Monica. From there, it was not far to Culver City, if you're the type who thinks in terms of miles. In terms of class, Culver City could have been at the other end of the universe. As I drove east on Washington Boulevard, the buildings became shabbier, the white stucco not quite so gleaming. Even the brilliant sunlight couldn't help.

The Acme Robot Company was a small square

building next to a big fenced-in yard. A not very en-
thusiastic box hedge ran along the wall on either side
of the brown door.

I parked out in front—parallel parking is a bitch,
not bitchen, just a bitch—and went to look through
the chain-link fence at the setup. There was a big truck
nosing a warehouse, and a van parked next to it, like
a mother and her young. On their sides, both had
ACME ROBOT COMPANY and a cartoon of a robot
who had a funnel for a hat. A thin black dog who had
been sleeping in the shade of the truck ran at me
barking and snarling as if it didn't know which to do
first. It stopped a few feet away from me and just
stared. Then it sat down and scratched itself.

I walked to the big brown door, opened it, and went
into a room that was so dark after the bright day that
for a moment I couldn't see a thing. The place smelled
of must and cardboard and old machinery—not an
unpleasant smell but also not one that would give a
customer confidence.

I stood by the door waiting for my eyes to adjust
when a voice said, "Can I help you with something,
maybe?" It was the voice of an old man, cautious but
not unkind. It was the type of voice you'd want to tell
you stories before you went to sleep at night.

I was in a stockroom. The floor had been swept
lately, but it would never be young again and it would
need more than sweeping to get up the cracks and
cigarette burns. Cardboard cartons were piled on top
of a long table that was pushed against one wall. More
cartons were stacked below it and to either side of it.
There were a lot of cartons that maybe had surf-bot
parts in them. The serial numbers on their sides
didn't tell me anything.

I took a step forward and saw that on the far side of the long table was a thin man sitting in a big leather chair whose color somehow matched the gloom around it. The thin man had straight black hair combed precisely back from his wide forehead. He wore a gray sweater that buttoned up the front and a pair of glasses in thick black frames. His pants had pleats. His shoes, which at the moment I could see the bottoms of, had been worked hard. For all I knew, they were as old as the floor. He was rubbing his eyes up under his glasses as if I had awakened him.

"I'd like to talk to somebody about surf-bots," I said.

"You can talk to me." He stood, and I saw that he was a little taller than Thumper, which meant that I came up to the middle button on his sweater. He walked into an office across from the long table and sat down behind one of the two desks. Both desks carried enough papers to show that real work was done on them, but on the desk the thin man sat behind was an old mechanical adding machine as well. "Now," he said, while he not quite stared at my nose. He was probably jealous. Before he saw me, he thought he had the biggest nose around.

I said, "I'm looking for surf-bot parts."

"I wish you luck," the man said, as if I would need it.

"Why is that?"

"Nobody in town has surf-bot parts. I know. I talk to people." He made a small gesture with one hand, vaguely indicating all the people he talked to.

I said, "Down at the beach, people are crying for surf-bot parts. A smart guy could make a lot of money."

"Gold is not all that glitters," he said. "What exactly is your interest in surf-bot parts? You don't look like a surfer." He peered at me over his glasses. "As a matter of fact, you don't look like *anybody* I ever saw before."

"Nobody knows the trouble I've seen," I said. I sat down in a wooden armchair in front of the desk. "I'm a private detective working for a client."

He nodded and said, "Trouble is your business."

"So far," I said. "And I haven't even started yet." I recognized that crack about trouble. It was the name of a book of short stories by Raymond Chandler. I said, "Me and Philip Marlowe."

He nodded again, only this time he smiled too. He was a very talented guy. "I like Chandler. His people don't shoot each other unless they mean it."

"And he knows how to squeeze a hyperbole till it screams."

"You got the patter down, anyway. What can I do for you?"

I said, "Not much happening at the Acme Robot Company."

"Not much happening at any robot company." He looked out the window for a while. Outside, traffic passed. An air compressor under the window began to chug. The gentle monotonous sound seemed to make a decision for him. He said, "SSR came around and bought up everything. Their representative said he'd be back to buy anything else we made."

"SSR?"

"You're really not a surfer, are you? SSR stands for Surfing Samurai Robots. They are the biggest manufacturer of surf-bots in the world. They make everything from a fancy model that just about surfs itself down to their cheap-o borax model, which you wind up with a big key."

"Key?"

"Just a joke." He shrugged. Jokes didn't concern him much.

"Why would an outfit like SSR buy your stock?"

"I couldn't tell you. But they paid retail. They really wanted that stuff."

I brandished a finger at him and said, "If I were in your place, I'd be turning out surf-bot parts night and day."

"Don't point that finger at me, young fellow," he said as he wagged his own finger in my direction. "Greed never pays." The old man shrugged. "Besides, I'm not getting any younger. I got everything I need. Why push my luck making SSR angry?"

"Robot parts are just kind of a hobby with you."

He nodded sagely.

I thought for a moment and said, "Either SSR is building an awful lot of robots, or they want to prevent everybody else from building robots."

"Could be both."

"Could be," I agreed. "Up in Malibu, there's a whole garage full of wrecked surf-bots. Without parts, they'll stay wrecked."

"Talk to SSR. I got plenty of nothing." He repeated, "Plenty of nothing," as if he liked the sound of the words.

I stood and looked toward the door. "Thanks, Mr.—?"

"Mr. Harold Chesnik, owner and operator of the Acme Robot Company."

"Thanks, Mr. Chesnik. You've been a big help."

He looked out the window. Nothing had changed

on the street. He said, "I'm not very busy. You are from someplace besides Los Angeles, I can tell."

"Bay City."

"Have it your way, Mr.—?"

"Marlowe," I said. "Zoot Marlowe." I looked him straight in the eye as I said it. He looked right back at me. His face did not even change expression. At last he said, "Well, Zoot, business, as you've noticed, is a little slow. I like you. I got time. I could maybe give you the Raymond Chandler tour of the city."

Time was running through my personal hourglass pretty quick. I had work to do. SSR was calling to me. The Surf-O-Rama was coming right up. So I said, "If you can dish it out, I can take it."

"You got the patter down," Mr. Chesnik said again. He chuckled as he shook his head. "You're a *real* tough guy."

CHAPTER 7
The Tour

Mr. Chesnik invited me out into the fenced-in yard. We walked through a garage to a door on the other side. The garage was crowded not only with ancient machine parts and tools but with heavy grease and the rancid spirits of heavy grease past.

Out in the shopworn sunshine, the dog barked as it gamboled over to us, tongue lolling. Evidently, anybody who was OK with the boss was OK with the dog. It stopped suddenly, a little farther away than I could spit, and backed away from me. It watched me closely but did not growl.

"Shame, Benny," Mr. Chesnik said. "Zoot here is a friend of mine."

Benny sat down and scratched himself vigorously behind one ear with a hind foot. Evidently, that's how he took care of a lot of problems. I'd try it myself if I thought it would do any good.

Mr. Chesnik's old Oldsmobile was parked on the far side of the Acme truck, where it couldn't be seen from the street. It was about the same vintage as my Chevy, but it had more buttons on the dash. "Genuine leather upholstery," he told me with some pride. The car's engine made about as much noise as a bumble-bee.

He took me to Hollywood by way of Beverly Hills. This was the long way around in anybody's map book, but I didn't doubt that it was the scenic route.

Washington Boulevard was a wide street with two-story buildings on either side of it and parking down the middle. Most buildings dripped with enough fili-gree to outfit a Gothic cathedral or two. Mr. Chesnik told me that nobody builds them like that anymore. "They build 'em like cheese boxes now. It's a style. Maybe someday they'll build them with knickknacks on the outside again." He really missed those knick-knacks.

We went north on La Cienega to Wilshire. A BMW cut us off as we passed under the Santa Monica Free-way. Mr. Chesnik braked sharply, almost sending us both through the windshield. He yelled some guttural words at the black car as it scuttled away. The words were not English, at least no English I had ever heard. He accelerated quickly to the next street and skidded to a stop at the red light.

"Mashuganah," he said as his fingers flexed on the steering wheel.

"If that means an accident looking for a place to happen, then you're right."

"I'm right." He breathed deeply, trying to relax. "*Mashuganah* means crazy."

"It's not English, is it?"

"Yiddish."

"What's that?"

Mr. Chesnik took a long look at me. You could have tap-danced on the cool strand that stretched between our eyes. He snapped it off when the light turned to green and, at the same moment, somebody behind us honked. The Oldsmobile began to move, but it wasn't Mr. Chesnik's jolly mood moving it. His mouth was firm. He said, "Bay City must be farther away than I thought."

"Probably," I said. "Far enough away that I sometimes need a little slack."

"Slack, I got plenty. But everybody runs out. Even me."

After a while, I said, "Tell me about Yiddish."

He spoke while we drifted past a lot of places selling car stereos and cellular phones. He told me about coming to the United States from a place called Latvia when he was just a kid and making good because he worked eighteen hours a day. "We spoke Yiddish at home because that's what Mom and Pop spoke. That was a long time ago, but I still see some of the old crowd. And you never forget the language you spoke as a kid."

I nodded, knowing he was right. I said, "Maybe Bay City isn't as far from here as either of us thinks."

"Could be," Mr. Chesnik said, but gently.

He turned left onto Wilshire Boulevard. Watching a good driver make a left turn was as satisfying as watching a trapeze artist work without a net.

As we rolled past the glass cheese boxes that so offended Mr. Chesnik, he began to talk about Chandler. Every time Mr. Chesnik said the name, I felt a twinge of excitement. I had found the main nerve—detective central.

Evidently, Chandler had been quite a drinker, and, to hear Mr. Chesnik tell it, he drank something stronger than brewski. Though Chandler worked for the movies, not many people liked his more-literary-

than-thou attitude. But Chandler was a fast boy with
a quip, Chandler was, and he told his associates, "Actually, I am just literary enough. If I were any worse
a writer, you would not have invited me. If I were any
better a writer, I would not have come." That quip and
a quarter will buy you a newspaper.

We passed the Beverly Wilshire Hotel, a flat-fronted
gray edifice. Hanging over the sidewalk were flags and
banners that decorated the building as subtly as
markings on a surfboard. Mr. Chesnik said, "In *The
Long Goodbye* Chandler called this place the Beverly
Ritz." I watched the place over my shoulder for a long
time as Mr. Chesnik drove on.

The traffic thickened as the average price of the
cars went up. Carefully dressed men and women drove
as if they knew that life would not surprise them with
anything they didn't want to surprise them. The shops
got smaller, but brass gleamed on their doors, and
tasteful awnings shaded their windows. There were a
lot of French names and cute puns. It was that sort of
neighborhood.

"Downtown Beverly Hills," Mr. Chesnik said.

"Los Angeles County's money clip."

Mr. Chesnik expelled some air that might have
been a laugh. We drove past Victor Hugo's Restaurant
and were a block or so away from a big white ghost of
a building that Mr. Chesnik identified as Beverly Hills
City Hall.

I said, "A place full of secrets and big money and
no more ethics than a pampered poodle." Marlowe had
never said that, but he could have. It had a nice ring.

From there we rolled up the hill at Doheny and
passed the spot where Mavis Weld's apartment used
to be, at least in *The Little Sister*. Mavis Weld was

Orfamay Quest's older sister. The one who was in pictures before she got in trouble. At Sunset, Mr. Chesnik turned right, and we rolled past strip joints and comedy clubs and places where you might be able to get a cup of coffee for a dollar or two if you had a good agent or weren't so thirsty that you couldn't wait half an hour.

We took La Brea up from Sunset to Franklin, passing through the disaster area that is still called Hollywood, but has nothing to do with the searchlight-and-satin fantasy I heard about on Lux Radio Theater.

Franklin was a clean street with big houses on either side. A few of them were protected by ivy-covered walls you couldn't see over. The ones that didn't have walls had columns like Greek temples and were so impressive, you'd want to wipe your feet just walking by.

Mr. Chesnik said, "Old General Sternwood of *The Big Sleep* lived around here somewhere. Remember, he had those two wild daughters? One of them was played by Lauren Bacall in the Bogart picture."

I nodded, having no idea who he was talking about. But I didn't say anything, figuring he had enough to think about for one day.

We pulled up in front of a house no bigger than most of them, which is to say, it was only two stories high and each member of the immediate family could have his or her own wing. But beyond that, it didn't resemble the other mansions in the neighborhood. More important, I couldn't place it in any of the Chandler stories I'd read or heard.

The house had no grace. It had been built by some rich man, but not to show the world he was rich. This was a place the rich man came to hide. It was a big stone block with a thing like a guard tower at each corner. They may have *been* guard towers for all I knew. Windows facing the street were no more than slits, the kind of thing from which Robin Hood might shoot arrows. The place looked as friendly as a penitentiary.

The house was an island of stone in the center of a grass ocean dotted at tasteful intervals with trees. A smooth curve of cement driveway swept by the front of the house and ducked under a big car the color of the inside of a rabbit's ear.

"This isn't part of the tour," Mr. Chesnik said, "but it might interest you."

"I'm fascinated already."

"If you can turn down the volume on the patter for just a moment, I'll tell you who this house belongs to."

I waited.

He said, "This house belongs to Knighten Daise, the owner of Surfing Samurai Robots."

I took another look at the house. Suddenly the day was a little darker. The house was no longer just a block of stone but a sinister fortress. A guy in a cloak and a mask lurked behind every corner and every tree.

I said, "Is it built like the Alamo to keep something in or something out?"

"I don't know. Mr. Daise don't confide in me very much."

We stared at the mansion for a while, but it didn't tell us anything. "Had enough?" Mr. Chesnik said.

I nodded and said, "If there are dungeons underground, I can't see them."

"Don't you folks in Bay City have X-ray vision?"

"What's an X ray?"

By this time it was just after noon. Clouds had

moved in from the ocean, elbowing each other like bumpkins while they mobbed over the city. Mr. Chesnik talked about somebody named Superman. Superman had X-ray vision. He could see through things. I told Mr. Chesnik that as far as I knew, nobody in Bay City had X-ray vision. He seemed disappointed and continued to shake his head while he fought his way through the traffic on Highland, slid over to La Brea and through a fairly nice area where apartment buildings were built as close together as slats in a fence.

On Venice Boulevard, Mr. Chesnik said, "Used to have a good rapid transit system here between the two directions of traffic. I could go anyplace on a Red Car."

"What happened?"

"Somebody thought it would be nice if they sold more cars."

At Acme Robots I unlocked the gate for Mr. Chesnik, then rode with him to the back of the yard. Benny was so glad to see us, he barked and leaped at Mr. Chesnik's window, festooning it with strings of dog spit. While the dog danced around us, we walked to the front of the yard, pushed the gate back into place, and locked it. It was the kind of neighborhood where that always would be a good idea.

Benny barked for a while after we went back into the office. Mr. Chesnik sat down behind his desk. I stood in the office doorway and said, "Thanks for the tour."

"You couldn't buy a tour like that," he said as he wiggled a finger at me.

"I guess I'm one lucky guy. If my luck holds out, you'll have the address of Surfing Samurai Robots."

He said nothing but backed away from the desk and fished around in the crowded center drawer until he came up with a card. From it he copied an address onto a scrap of paper and handed it over. On the paper was the printed legend, "Get Your Grommets from Comet." Sounded like a plan.

By this time Benny had given up barking, probably in favor of scratching. While Mr. Chesnik and I shook hands, I said, "If you hear anything interesting about surf-bots, give me a call." I tore an even smaller scrap from the bottom of the scrap he'd given me and wrote the phone number of the house in Malibu on it. He threw it into the center drawer and pushed the drawer closed with his stomach.

"Hell of a filing system," I said.

He shrugged and said, "It works."

After pondering the map book for a few minutes, I was out of there and driving back to Hollywood. Traffic was heavier than it had been, and I was not as good a driver as Mr. Chesnik. I played touch-and-go up Highland and at last hit the Hollywood Freeway, where I ran into lumps of traffic as thick and inexplicable as the lumps in Whipper Will's yoyogurt.

I found Surfing Samurai Robots at last. It was a vast two-story building in the middle of an even vaster parking lot. To one side was an empty lot where high grass partly obscured a sign offering the land for sale. On the other side was another parking lot and another building and another For Sale sign. The parking lot was empty. I parked there and watched people come in and out of the Surfing Samurai Robot building, wondering how I would do the same.

CHAPTER 8
No Admittance

When I got out of the car, heat struck me like the palm of an enormous hand. I stood up to it, and I was tempted to leave my trench coat in the car but decided against it. The trench coat was part of the uniform. I compromised by folding the trench coat over my arm and pushing my hat back on my head.

That sweaty palm kept me in its grip all the way across the parking lot. If that wasn't bad enough, the smell of hot asphalt nearly strangled me. The guard at the front of the SSR parking lot didn't see me because he was busy with somebody in a big white car so shiny it hurt my eyes to look at it.

I wasn't interested in cars anyway. I peered under my hand through the double glass doors into the SSR lobby. A couple came out. The woman was tall and wore shoes that made her even taller and a short green dress that matched the shoes. The man wore a gray suit and a dark tie that was so thin he needn't have bothered with it. The man said something, and the woman laughed. It was a nice laugh, but none too sincere. I wondered if these were the people I was up against.

Before the door swung to a stop, I was inside the
lobby and glad I'd kept my trench coat. The lobby was
a big marble box filled with the echoes of people talking earnestly and walking across the smooth floor as
if getting somewhere else were important. Most of
them were dressed more or less in the style of the two
I had met at the door. Everybody has a uniform. The
room was cold enough to stiffen my nose, but it was
just right to impress people coming in from the heat
outside, if you impress easily.

I walked to the building directory and studied it as
if I knew who I was looking for. A man in a gray uniform walked up to me and said, "Can I help you, sir?"

The man had no interest in helping me. He was
not quite as old as Mr. Chesnik, and he was cut from
different cloth. He had a hard look to him. There was
no expression in his face, but his eyes would never
believe anything. Some of his belly rode over the top
of his wide black belt. He was probably a retired cop
trying to fill out his pension with a couple of extra
bucks. I wondered if his gun was loaded and decided
it would be, just for the sake of pride.

"Sure. Uh, thanks. I'm looking for the showroom.
I'd like to buy a robot."

"Yes, sir." The face could have been made from the
same marble as the lobby. It wasn't built to smile.
"Just there, sir," he said as he pointed across the lobby
to more glass doors.

I tipped my hat to him and set off, feeling his eyes
prodding me the whole way. I pushed through a glass
door that had You Can Depend on an SSR Robot
stamped on it in gold. The room beyond was not much
smaller than the lobby, but it was warm enough that
my nose thawed a little and began to itch.

There were a lot of robots in the room, everything from big muscular galoots, that might have been human if their muscles hadn't been molded out of golden metal, down to little buggers that looked like mechanical can openers. The one thing each of them had in common was a cloth band tied around its head.

I turned around, looking for the source of a strong, harsh smell, and found a kid not much older than Thumper polishing a silver beachball that had legs and octopus arms. He spit on the thing and polished it vigorously. From the gleam of every piece in the room, spitting and polishing was a full-time job. It was the polish that smelled, not the kid.

Despite the number of robots standing around, the room was not crowded. Scattered among the robots were hooded television sets showing SSR robots in action and big display boards listing features. Posters on the walls were paintings of the most expensive robots serving drinks and playing tennis. Light and shadow, all very artistic. Not one of the posters showed a robot surfing.

A slim guy in a pinstripe suit hurried over to me. You could have cut cheese with the crease in his pants. He was the guy the suit salesman at For Men Only wanted to be when he grew up. He smiled at me and rubbed his hands together and said, "Good morning, sir. What can I do for you?" He didn't quite lick his lips. The guy was good. Even after he got a close look at me, his smile slipped only a little.

In a polite voice I hadn't used since leaving T'toom, I said, "I'm looking for a surf-bot."

That shocked him. He saw big-nosed, white-skinned fellows from T'toom every day, but my question about surf-bots made his eyes wander and the smile go where smiles go. He said, "I'm afraid we're a little short of surf-bots right now. Could I interest you in something else? A robotler, perhaps?"

"Maybe I better talk to another salesman."

"You can't do better than talking to me," he said as brightly as a new tin spoon. "I've been salesman of the month three months in a row." He pointed to where a row of photographs defaced the wall. One of the photographs was of him, with a big paper star taped over it.

"I see," I said, hoping I sounded impressed. "Then maybe *you* can answer a question for me." I made it sound like a question men had waited a thousand years to have answered by some oracle on a mountaintop.

"If I can."

"What the hell is a surfing samurai robot?"

He opened his face and made a big hearty laugh. I smiled politely, just to be one of the guys. He handed me a sheet of paper that was almost as slick as he was. The paper told me again why an SSR robot was the best. At the top it said, "Surfing Samurai Robots: The Agility of a Surfer and the Devotion of a Samurai." That explained a lot—except that I didn't know what a samurai was. According to the salesman, they wore headbands, just like the SSR robots.

Lance—he insisted I call him Lance—spent a lot of time showing me around the showroom. He acted as if he were showing off his children. A high point that Lance was unaware of was a door marked NO ADMITTANCE. I leaned against it and felt it give.

There was not one surf-bot in the place. Lance said they were waiting on a shipment. He frowned. "We've been waiting for a while." The wait seemed to bother him. If he was faking, he was damned good at it. Of course, he would be.

All those robots gave me ideas. I asked good ol' Lance if he had a companion robot that knew the Los Angeles area. "Just the thing," he said and showed me a little silver jobber that looked like a duck. Its name was Bill. "Get it?" Lance said, not quite prodding me in the ribs with an elbow, "Duck? Bill? Duck bill?"

While I nodded over the mechanical duck, thinking about how useful it might be, Lance asked me how I would pay for it.

The question was a good one and quick enough, it stopped me nodding. I had a hundred bucks in my pocket that would not go very far if I spent it all in one place. I had no credit rating anywhere on Earth. Before I knew what I was doing, I said, "I believe Mr. Chesnik of Acme Robots has a commercial account with you." I tried not to show my surprise when this came out of my mouth.

After that, there were a lot of phone calls—from Lance to the Credit Department, from the Credit Department to Mr. Chesnik, and at last from Mr. Chesnik to me.

He said, "You got your nerve."

"If I don't use it, it rusts," I said.

He chuckled without mirth. It might have been his chair squeaking. He said, "I shouldn't do this."

"If you didn't intend to do this, why talk to me?"

"Always the patter. OK. I'll take a chance. Can you really pay for the robot?"

"Call that number I gave you. Talk to a guy named Whipper Will."

"I seem to be doing you a lot of favors."

"I noticed. Thanks."

"Smart mouth," he grumbled and hung up.

A moment later, the Credit Department called and gave Lance the OK. Lance went into high gear. He filled out a lot of papers. I signed them quickly, trying to make it look as if I'd signed papers before. I gave the surf house in Malibu as my address. Lance said that Bill would be delivered there in a few days. We shook hands. It was all very gentlemanly.

Now that our business was concluded, Lance was eager to be off to his next challenge. I said, "I'd like to look around a bit more."

"Sure," he said, his mind already on the meek couple glancing around from the center of the room. "Let me know if you see anything else you like." He laughed and shook my hand again, and then, was trotting toward the meek couple with no more thought of me than what a bee has for its last flower.

I wandered around the room, fiddled with the ball-and-socket joint exhibit, asked a computer some questions I didn't care to know the answers to, always moving toward the NO ADMITTANCE door. Nobody watched me. I was boring. I had already bought something and was not likely to buy anything else.

Then I slid through the door and was in a short hallway painted an institutional green. It was full of dead unmoving air. At the end of the hall was another door, also not locked. Beyond it, a wide hallway carpeted with a somber burgundy pattern crossed in front of me. The door I looked out of was just one of many. I stepped into the hallway, not knowing what I was looking for, but hoping to find it before somebody noticed my tie was too wide.

I heard a buzzing far off, but getting closer. I kept

walking but stopped abruptly when three small bi-wing airplanes banked around the corner and flew in formation down the hallway toward me.

I watched them in fascination. Without even slowing down, one of them casually used a red pencil of sparkling light to zap a white Styrofoam coffee cup that stood out like a welt on the burgundy carpet. The cup disappeared in a puff of vapor. The planes had nearly reached me. I backed against the wall, hoping that I was not on their list of things to zap. They circled in front of me like buzzards.

I ducked under the planes and ran down the hall. The planes flew after me, buzzing louder now as if they were angry. I turned the corner and saw a crowd of men in suits coming toward me. Being involved in manly conversation, they did not notice me, but it would not be long before they did. I looked back. The biplanes still wanted me. I backed into the first door I came to.

I leaned against the inside of the door, breathing hard. I inhaled the smell of humans, with a strong overlay of something chemical that was too sweet. It bit into the passages of my nose. I was in a long room covered in tile a lighter shade of the color of the burgundy carpeting outside. Along one side of the room were white fixtures. Along the other were some gray cubicles. The whole place bounced hard light around, not letting it rest. I walked to the only fixture I recognized, which was a sink. I splashed some cold water onto my face, then drank some of it from a cupped hand. It was exactly what I wanted.

I needed a place to think and went into one of the cubicles, where I found a toilet. So this was what a bathroom in an office building looked like. I waited for the crowd outside to break up. Time crawled by on its hands and knees.

Suddenly voices came into the room and exploded against the hard walls. I looked through the crack between the door of the cubicle and the molding and saw gray business suits. Big help. Water began to run.

"I don't like this," a voice said. If it had been deeper, I would have called it squeaky.

"We're close," the second voice said. "But we have to play out the game to the end."

"I don't even like robots," the first voice said.

"I forgot how delicate you are. But we'll take a look at them anyway," the second voice said. It was not an idle suggestion. There was menace in the voice.

A third voice, more of a grunt than a voice, said, "Yeah. Could be interesting to see how they get made."

I flushed the toilet and opened the door of the cubicle. Three pairs of liquid brown eyes glanced at me, as interested as if I were a fly buzzing in the corner. They looked away, intent on their own business.

While I washed my hands I studied the room's reflection in the mirror above the sink. The three who'd been talking wore suits all right, but if they were men then so was I. Everything not covered by suit was covered with coarse fur that was neither black nor brown but some dirty color in between. More than anything else, they looked like small gorillas.

But I forgave them that. I'd forgive them a lot more before I gave up on them. When they lumbered from the bathroom, going to see how robots were made, I followed.

CHAPTER 9
The Biplanes of Samson Andelilah

Except for the gorilla men ambling away from the bathroom, the hallway was empty. I followed them as closely as I dared, hoping that anyone who looked would think I was part of their group. Durf! Three gorillas and a geek. What must SSR be coming to?

A door opened and a female voice said, "I'll get these to him right away," and a short lumpy woman with a topknot of gray hair backed into the hall. She gave a quiet yelp when she saw us through her thick glasses, but only blinked a time or two and tried to kick-start a smile before she walked quickly in the direction from which we had come.

We kept moving, but we weren't in any hurry. Just three gorillas and a geek walking jaunty jolly. We rounded a corner and I saw one lonely biplane flying toward us from the far end of the hall. The gorillas slowed down, watchful.

"What'll we do, Spike?" the grunting voice said.

Spike said, "Just keep moving. We belong here, remember?" Even when he was being reassuring, Spike sounded as if he were making a threat.

The biplane quickly closed the space between us,

and I thought it would go on its way, but it began to circle us. The gorillas watched warily, ducking away from the plane, though it never came close enough for any of us to reach, not even the gorillas, each of whom had a reach like, um, a gorilla.

"Who are you?" Spike said. He'd taken a quick, surprised look at me, but he was watching the biplane again. We all were.

"Just somebody with an interest in robots," I said.

"Yeah?" he said, unconvinced.

I blew hard at the biplane. It sputtered and tumbled backward, almost hitting the far wall before it righted itself. It zagged and flew away, looking a little hurt, I thought.

"Pretty good," Spike said, "but it buys you exactly nothing."

"I heard you talking in the bathroom, and I thought I'd come along."

The one with the squeaky voice said, "He looks like some kinda freak too."

"Birth defect," I said. "I hear Mom took a lot of drugs in the sixties." I looked hard at the squeaky wheel and said, "What's your story?"

He reacted as if I'd kicked him in the stomach. Spike and the other gorilla laughed under their whiskers.

The squeaky one started to say something, and Spike said, "Shut up." The object of Spike's suggestion stuck out his chin like a football lineman ready for the snap but said nothing. Spike led his friends along the hall again. I walked too. Nobody told me I shouldn't. As we walked, a rhythmic thrumming got louder. Pretty soon, it filled the hallway, so thick you could almost swim in it.

The hallway dead-ended at a metal door. Spike pushed a thing the size of a credit card into a slot next to it, and a buzzer went off. The door snicked open, and the thrumming immediately became louder. We went inside to meet it. The door snicked closed behind us, sounding more definite about it than I would have liked. The buzzer stopped.

Beyond the door, arms, legs, torsos, and heads were everywhere. The pieces moved along conveyer belts or hung from hooks attached to tracks that snaked through the air just above head level. The walls were covered with patterns of lights that constantly changed. Guys in long white coats walked along looking at the walls and writing things on clipboards. I heard wind blowing somewhere, but I could not feel it. The room was no warmer than the lobby, but it also had no smell. For the first time since I'd come to Earth, my nose rested. It was stiff, but it rested.

The body parts were all made of metal, of course, and had wires and electrical plugs sticking out of them. They were just so many parts of a jigsaw puzzle at the moment. And the funny thing was who was putting the puzzle together: more robots. Robots building robots. The mind boggled. The construction robots made no sound. They just worked. The only sound in that place was the constant wind. The door behind us buzzed, and we all turned to look at who'd come in.

The door was just shutting behind two security guards. They were dressed like the old hard case in the lobby, but they had shiny silver faces that glinted in the bright light of the factory. Their hands were silver gauntlets. Though neither of them was bigger than the average human, their bulk made them seem huge. Machine intelligence shone behind each of their eyes like an electric bulb, and their right hands hung loose and ready near their pistols. In a voice that boomed from the bottom of a deep well, one of them said, "Excuse me."

Spike, ever the diplomat, said, "We ain't done nothing."

"This is a security area, sir. You'll have to come with us." The damned thing actually managed to make that hollow boom sound sorry.

"We got our rights," the gorilla with the squeaky voice said.

"Shut up, Tiger," Spike said.

The robot security guards walked us out of there, and we were joined by a squadron of biplanes. The planes and the security guards escorted us down the hall and into an elevator. The planes stayed behind, just circling in front of the elevator till the doors closed. The guards never actually touched us, but we knew we were caught. It was in the air like the heat outside.

The elevator took us down two floors and let us out into a cement corridor with pipes and conduits in the ceiling. The place smelled like fresh paint and hummed with power.

We turned right along the hallway and passed metal doors with numbers stenciled onto them. The door at the end of the hall had a glass window with chicken wire in it—pretty classy for this neighborhood. One of the robot guards opened the door for us while the other herded us into the small office beyond. As soon as the door was opened, I could smell stale cigarette smoke. Once inside the room, the smell was almost overwhelming.

There was thin green carpeting on the floor that was just enough different from the color of the walls to make your teeth hurt. On the walls were dull paintings or prints of paintings in dull frames. In the corner was a dusty rubber plant that was too big for its pot.

The largest man I ever saw sat behind a desk. Only that particular man could make that particular desk look like a toy. I don't know where they got a uniform to fit him. He took a puff of a cigarette and, with regret, laid it in the wire holder of a badly chipped ceramic ashtray. As if we had spittle on our chins, he studied us through the rising thread of smoke. The guards stood by the door, not moving any more than you would expect a metal man to move.

A nose the size of mine can be a terrific asset. Just taking a couple of polite sniffs can sometimes tell you things that you could not find out any other way. But right now, I wished I had a pug, like an Earthman. The cigarette smoke excavated the passages inside my nose as if it were looking for something. It didn't find anything and kept looking.

The big man said, "I am Samson Andelilah, head of SSR security. You gentlemen are in a great deal of trouble." If a French horn could talk, it would sound like that. It was a voice that grabbed you by the ears—funny, since I didn't have ears—and forced you to listen to it.

Spike said, "We was just looking around."

"You was all just looking around?" He picked up his cigarette and puffed calmly at me. I was the odd man out, not having enough fur on my body to make a coat for a flea.

I said, "I came in to buy a robot. I bought one. I guess I got lost on the way out."

The man behind the desk smiled.

Spike said, "Yeah. We got lost too."

"You need a card key to get into that assembly room."

"We come in the back way," Spike said. His explanation sounded thin, even to me, and I wanted Mr. Andelilah to believe it.

The phone rang. Still smiling, Andelilah picked up the receiver and listened. The smile went away, and he became kind of thoughtful. He nodded and said, "Yes, sir." Later, he said thank you and hung up.

"You three," he said, "can go." He drew a squiggle in the air with cigarette smoke.

I said, "At last count, there were four of us here."

"The three of you, get out of here. And keep your noses clean. You might not be so lucky again."

The two guards at the door stepped aside as the three gorillas nodded and shuffled out the door like bad boys leaving the principal's office. They didn't even look at me as they went out.

"Sit down," Andelilah said.

I pulled up a folding chair and sat down. I said, "Those guys must have something I don't know about. As far as I can tell, their only claim to fame is that they walk upright."

Andelilah nodded. That was exactly what he was expecting me to say. He meditated on me for a while and said, "You don't look like an industrial spy. Of course, the best ones never do." He spoke out loud, but he was speaking to himself. I just happened to be there. I waited.

"What? No protest?"

I said, "Would there be any point to a protest?"

"No."

"You were awfully easy on my hairy friends."

"I'm the trusting sort." Andelilah stubbed out the cigarette and waited a whole three seconds before he couldn't stand it anymore and lit up another one.

"The one who did all the talking had the card key on him. Where I come from we call that evidence."

"Where exactly do you come from?"

"Bay City."

"That a place on Mars?" He looked at me hard, eyebrows up, waiting for the big revelation.

I shifted in my seat and said, "We could sit here and crack wise at each other all day. When it's time for you to go home, I could see the changing of the guard."

"We're just biding our time."

"Biding?"

"Our time. Somebody wants to see you, and he's not quite ready yet."

"I've met guys in their stocking feet before."

Andelilah lowered his cigarette hand and laughed out loud.

I said, "Terrific. I have the house in the palm of my hand. Listen, Andelilah, you know I didn't see anything worth seeing in that assembly room. If I had, those gorillas would have seen it too and you never would have let them go."

"What you saw or did not see is no longer the point."

The telephone rang, and both of us jumped. My chair creaked as I leaned back in it. The phone rang again, and Andelilah reached for it. He listened for a moment, said, "Right away," and replaced the receiver gently. To the robot guards he said, "Take him to the interviewing room."

It was a line from a movie, but I didn't think it was a joke. Each of the guards grabbed an arm and pulled me to my feet. Through my trench coat and suit I could feel their hard fingers.

As if I were a problem he had not yet solved, Andelilah watched me while the guards pulled me from the room. The air in the corridor was more or less clean. It was a pleasure to get out there and breathe.

I thought Samson Andelilah's office was in the basement, but there was at least one floor even lower. The guards took me down to it. When the elevator doors opened, I was looking down a short corridor. More concrete, more conduits and pipes. At the end of the corridor was a wooden door. A regular wooden door. Then I noticed that it didn't have a doorknob.

We stood in front of the door, and a moment later it slid aside. As we walked through the doorway I could see that the wood was only a layer on the outside. The rest of the door was as thick and complicated as the door of the airlock back on the *Philip Marlowe*. The door slid shut behind us. I said, "Now what?"

There was no answer. I turned around and saw that I was alone. I was in a room with a huge dark window at one end, a wide slot under the window and an easy chair in the middle of the room. I walked to the window and looked through it under one hand. The other side was darker than the inside of Grampa Zamp's left nostril.

It was obvious that I was supposed to sit in the easy chair, so I went to a corner of the room and crouched there, watching for something, anything that would give me a clue about where I was and what would happen next.

I sniffed and smelled the ocean. I heard the gentle lapping of what might have been waves and an uneven clicking noise that started and stopped, started and then stopped for a long time. I got the impression that something on the other side of the glass was looking at me.

A loud electronic click filled the room. The gentle lapping sound was louder, as if it were now being amplified. A thin, scratchy voice from my worst nightmares spoke. It said, "Good morning, Mr. Marlowe."

CHAPTER 10
Knighten Daise, You Are the One

I said, "Good morning. I guess you got my name from Lance in sales." My voice wobbled like a kid learning to ride a two-wheeler.

"I would prefer not to say."

Ignoring the voice, I went on, "Which means that you are pretty high up in this company or work for someone who is."

There was a long silence while the owner of the voice made a decision. Waves came in and went out. At last the voice said, "Mr. Marlowe, you have been brought here because I need some help."

"At the moment, I need some help myself."

The voice grumbled to itself, scratching like the spiral at the end of a phonograph record. It said, "We are not here to discuss your problems."

"Terrific. Then I'll just be going." I got to my feet and stood in front of the door. It was a bluff. There was no way that door was going to open just yet.

The nightmare voice said again, "I need help." A moment later it added, "And I thought you might give it to me."

"Who exactly are you?"

"That is of no consequence."

"It's of consequence to me if you want me to help you."

"You are a detective, are you not? You are in the business of helping people."

"How did you know I was a detective?"

"It is obvious."

The uniform, sure. I turned from the door and sat down in the easy chair. If they were going to hurt me, it could be done anywhere in the room. A spray of machine gun bullets or some funny gas would do it. The chair was comfortable. My voice was steady when I said, "Do you always hire the first detective who walks into your building?"

"Timing," the voice said, "is everything."

"So I'm lucky. But I don't do business with mystery clients. There is enough mystery in my life without that."

Water continued to lap at a phantom beach. I took a deep breath through my nose. The smell of the sea tickled it and worked at flushing out the cigarette smoke—an uphill battle.

"You may call me Mr. Daise."

"Is that who you are?"

"Yes, as far as you're concerned. Listen, Mr. Marlowe, my identity really has nothing to do with the service I want you to perform."

"Is that why you're hiding behind that dark glass?"

"What makes you think I'm hiding?"

I laughed.

"I have many enemies, Marlowe. I didn't build this room just to meet with you."

"I suppose that's good enough for the moment. What is the service?"

"I am looking for a missing person."

"Call the police."

"The police refuse to help just yet. They need to wait a week after the missing-person report is filed, or they need a ransom note, whichever comes first. Mr. Marlowe, I fear my daughter has been kidnapped, and I want her back *now*."

The voice wasn't so bad once I got used to it. Only the initial shock of hearing that near-human insect voice was terrifying. If it had been entirely human or entirely nonhuman, I could have handled it. It was the not *quite* human part that made the voice so awful. Strange sentiments from a guy who was not of this Earth. But I'd been listening to human voices for a long time before I got to Earth, and had had a chance to get used to them. Besides, neither birds nor crickets make human sounds, yet humans will pay a lot of money to go where they can be heard. To me, human voices had a pleasant natural sound. I don't know what I sounded like to humans, but I hadn't had any complaints.

A big envelope fell through the slot to the floor. "Here is a photograph of my daughter, Heavenly."

I picked up the envelope and unwound some red string to get it open. Inside was a photograph of a young woman with a curly explosion of rust-red hair. She was wearing a brief purple swimsuit that might have been sprayed on and did not leave much to the imagination. A bucket holding a champagne bottle and some crushed ice stood within easy reach. Also within easy reach was a tall golden robot with the trademark SSR band around its forehead. It was carrying a surfboard. Golden muscles rippled perfectly, the way only metal muscles can.

I said, "Who's the tin can?"

I'd stepped on the voice's toes. It said, "*That* is hardly a tin can, Mr. Marlowe. It is SSR's best model, and it is fully functional. Among other things, it actually surfs, which many SSR models do not do."

"If it's still fully functional, it's the only surf-bot around that is."

"What does that mean?" the voice said angrily. Did Mr. Daise just not like me to steer the conversation, or had I ever so delicately touched a nerve?

"Maybe nothing," I said. "What does it mean to you?"

"Why, nothing whatsoever. What is your fee?"

Philip Marlowe had gotten twenty-five a day plus expenses. But that had evidently been a long time ago. The prices in the mall in Malibu had been an education. I said, "A hundred a day, plus expenses." Mr. Daise said, "Fine. You can pick up a week's retainer at the reception desk on your way out." He said it very quickly, and I knew I should have asked for more.

I said, "Tell me about Heavenly."

"We have never been as close as a father and his daughter ought to be. I suggest you interview the Daise social secretary, Sylvia Woods. I will tell her to expect you."

"For a father who's not close you seem awfully worried about Heavenly."

"A father and daughter don't have to be joined at the hip in order to worry about one another."

"Right you are." I stood up and waved my finger around, taking in the nearly empty room and most particularly the dark glass window. I said, "This is a hell of a setup."

"I earned my comforts *and* the right not to be

judged by you, Mr. Marlowe. When I started this company back in '65, I was the only one making robots because I was the only one who knew how." His chuckle was like gravel falling through a sifter. "I was going to call them Asimov's Choice, but I wasn't quick enough to pick up the rights. It was one of the few mistakes I've made in my life. Even now I'm a better engineer than any three chip-meisters graduating from school today. I ought to know. I hire enough of them."

Carrying the photo inside its envelope, I walked to the door and waited. I said, "It's been nice talking to you, Mr. Daise, but it's turning out to be a rather full afternoon. . . ." I let my thought dangle in midair, which is all it deserved.

"Have you noticed that I have not yet told you where the Daise mansion is? Maybe I should have waited for another private detective to come into my building after all."

"You hired the right private detective, Mr. Daise. I have ways to find out where you live." A moment later the door slid open. The two guards were waiting for me outside. As we walked to the elevator I said, "Good-looking gent, Mr. Daise is."

Neither of the guards said anything.

As Mr. Daise had promised, there was a check for five hundred dollars waiting for me at the reception desk in the lobby. Sitting behind the desk was a young girl who had a lot of dark elaborate hair and was wearing a white dress decorated with blue and pink palm trees. She handed the envelope to me along with a big smile that almost succeeded in raising the temperature in the lobby. The security guard glanced at us, just to keep his hand in, and then went back to his real work—rocking on his heels and staring at the tall grass in the field next door.

I asked the receptionist where I could make a phone call, and she directed me to a telephone on an end table nearby. I sat in a chair that was a lot less comfortable than it looked and dialed Malibu.

After six rings a male voice answered, and I asked for Whipper Will. The male voice didn't say anything, but I heard the receiver drop on the floor and leisurely footsteps of the voice's owner walk away. I waited. The grass in the lot next door grew higher. The smile on the receptionist was a little overripe now when she looked my way. As far as the security guard was concerned, I had been in the lobby long enough to qualify as another piece of furniture.

Brisk footsteps approached the phone and Whipper Will said, "Hello?"

"I thought I was going to have to crawl through the phone and find you myself."

"Hello, Zoot."

I told him about how I'd gone to see Mr. Chesnik and how he had put me onto Surfing Samurai Robots. Whipper Will said a drawn out, "Oh," as if the mention of SSR made a lot of things clearer. Then he said, "You've had a busy morning. You think SSR is behind all this?"

"Maybe. But that still doesn't explain Gotterdammerung's interest, if any, or even why SSR might be bothering to destroy surf-bots. They can't need the small amount of business you might give them when all of this is over."

"No." The sound of waves breaking on the shore hissed delicately over the phone. I thought of Mr. Daise behind his black window. I said, "What is a samurai, anyway?"

Whipper Will laughed his laugh and said, "A kind of Japanese soldier that was very loyal to the dude giving the orders."

"Handy for the dude giving the orders. Are SSR robots really that good?"

"So I hear. Personally, I like to build my surf-bots from a kit."

"Sure. You're all fingers."

"What?"

"All fingers. Isn't that the opposite of all thumbs?"

"Evidently only in Bay City."

"That story's wearing a little thin, is it?"

"I'll believe it till you say different."

"Thanks." I hung up thinking about the strange places I found friends. The envelope with the check inside felt good against my ribs. It reminded me that I'd forgotten to tell Whipper Will I could start paying my own way.

When I opened the door of the Belvedere hot air punched me like a wad of damp cotton. I climbed into the oven, rolled down the front windows on either side of the car, and let what wind there was blow through while I checked the water pistol in the glove compartment. It had leaked a little, but it still put out a good shot when I tried it against the hot cement of the empty parking lot. The water disappeared immediately when it hit the ground. I put the pistol into an outside suit coat pocket.

Traffic had not improved. Automobiles seemed to have paired off and had big litters while I was inside SSR. I wound slowly down between the Hollywood Hills and into Hollywood itself. Somebody rode my tail until I followed the snake dance at the Highland exit. The car that had ridden my bumper so hard rolled forward one car's length and hugged the bumper of the car that had been in front of me. Some people might call that progress.

Between two cheap hotels that had despondent black men sitting out front like gargoyles, I found a place that sold hamburgers. The smell inside the small one-story building was thick enough to carve and gave the impression of having been there a long time.

Most of the people ahead of me in line ordered a burger, a shake, and some fries. I used a little of the money Whipper Will had given me that morning to do the same. At a tiny yellow table barely large enough for me to set out my food I took a bite and discovered the flavors were powerful—solid versions of the smells— but unlike anything I'd had before, even on Earth. A lot of people were eating there, so it must have been a good place, but the food made the back of my throat tickle, and my stomach was trying to send it back.

I made the short drive over to Franklin, where the traffic at this hour moved faster than the traffic on the freeway. I stopped the car in front of the Daise mansion. Traffic slid by, cool and serene on its way to put another few bones down the city's throat.

The Daise mansion looked no more inviting than it had that morning when Mr. Chesnik had shown it to me. The pale gray car was still in the driveway. I got out of my Chevy and walked to the gate, feeling better for the exercise. The gate was made of the same wrought iron spears as the rest of the fence. A small child could have squeezed between those spears. I probably could have done it myself. Instead, I pushed a pearl button on a small box next to the gate and waited for an answer.

CHAPTER 11
A Nasty Idea

I was expected. The voice that answered the squawker was professional but almost friendly. The gate swung open as if it were part of a fairy tale, and I walked up the driveway. If that guy behind the black window wasn't Mr. Daise, he was the next best thing.

It was a nice driveway, and I liked walking on it, but things kept flickering on either side of me. When I looked in the direction of the flickers, all I saw were trees moving casually in the breeze. That hadn't been what I'd seen. Then one of the flickers got careless and I saw a uniformed man duck behind a tree. After that, I spotted three more uniformed men. But they weren't ducking behind those trees. The trees were fake, each one a sentry box for one of those guards. They said nothing to me, and I said nothing to them. I was expected.

The big car in front of the house had a fine layer of dust on it. I looked through the window at the steering wheel and saw that it had a layer of dust on it too. While I was looking, someone coughed.

I straightened up and looked across the hood of the car to the front entrance, which was carved out of

two gigantic slabs of dark wood. The twin doors had
opened inward. Standing in the space between them
with one hand politely covering his mouth was a robot the color of a new penny. He was dressed in a
white shirt and soft gray pants. Around his head was
an SSR headband. His expression was unreadable.

I said, "I didn't know robots coughed."

"Coughing can be a useful social noise, sir." The
robot had the friendly professional voice I'd heard on
the box down at the gate. I walked over to the doors,
and he said, "Ms. Woods is expecting you."

As I passed through, I said, "What about those guys
outside?"

Those guys were not a surprise to him. He didn't
even stutter when he said, "They have been fully
briefed. If they had not been, your visit would have
already ended. One way or another." The robotler may
have smiled.

The penitentiary look of the place was only skin
deep. I followed the robotler into a two-story foyer
with a second-floor hallway looking down at it over a
banister wide enough for road racing. Tapestries of
unicorns and very polite dragons hung from the side
walls, and behind me was a rose window God Himself
would have been proud to own. High-backed wooden
chairs with red seats stood at intervals along the foyer,
and between them were doors. The wood in the chairs
and the doors had the look of an old musical instrument.

The robotler led me into a room off the foyer that
must have been a library, or one of the libraries. *A*
through *G*, maybe. The volumes were as old as they
looked—I could smell the paper. I wondered if Mr.
Daise had bought them by the yard, or if anybody had

ever read them. Bisecting the center of the room was a long leather couch. A pattern of concentric circles was already disappearing from one of the cushions.

The robot said, "Ms. Woods will be with you shortly." He walked out without making a sound and closed the door behind with a click. A grandfather clock stood in one corner of the room, slicing off the seconds while dust drifted through a shaft of yellow sunlight that fell in through a high window.

A woman came into the room. She wore a gray shirt open at the throat and jeans with high-heeled pumps peeking from under the narrow cuffs. Her red hair was pulled back into a ponytail. That, and the big glasses with the dark frames, made her look like a high-school kid on her first job. I knew her from someplace. And it wasn't just because all Earthpeople look alike to me. She held out her hand and told me that she was Sylvia Woods, the Daises' social secretary. "I didn't know when to expect you. But I thought it would take you longer to get this address."

"I told Mr. Daise I had my ways."

"The address and phone number are unlisted."

"That's right," I said. "I do it with mirrors."

"All right. I suppose you have some right to your professional secrets." She settled behind a desk big enough for basketball, wrinkled her nose, and looked at me as if she might know me too. She said, "Mr. Daise told me that I would not mistake you for anyone else, and he was right."

I told her what my wayward mom had done in the sixties and she made sympathetic noises.

"Have we met before?" I said.

She laughed. It was a nice laugh, a cadenza by Mozart. She said, "Mr. Daise said he showed you a picture of Heavenly. Some people say we could be sisters, but I never saw the resemblance. Heavenly's so pretty."

"Fishing?" I said.

"Compliments are always welcome." She smiled. It was enough to make me forget the grease churning in my stomach.

"You have them," I said. "And it's a pleasant surprise. Somehow I expected the Daise social secretary to be a robot."

"I'll tell you about that if you can keep a secret."

"I'm good at keeping secrets. But sometimes, all on their own, they leap out of their hidey-holes waving flags in the air."

"Not this one. And to answer your next question, no, it has nothing to do with Heavenly's disappearance."

"Oh? Are there suddenly two detectives in here?"

She smiled. "All right. It's just this: Privately, Mr. Daise believes that humans have a touch that robots lack."

"A human touch."

"Yes. Some very sophisticated robots have intuition circuits that give them something that looks like social grace. But it's the social grace of a monkey waving bye-bye or a dog shaking hands."

"And yet Mr. Daise has a robotler."

"Sure. Robots are more reliable than humans. And nobody expects or even wants servants to have feelings."

"Besides," I said, "samurai robots don't drink the sherry while the master is away or hock the family silver."

While she was nodding, I said, "Tell me about Heavenly."

She leaned back in the huge leather chair and shook her head as she began to push a pencil around on the green blotter. "Poor Heavenly. She always wanted to be normal. Her friends had terrific tans and hung out at the mall and ate sushi and drove their BMWs and drank the right wine while they sat in their hot tubs. Most of them never had a thought in their pastel lives. But Heavenly was too smart to be normal. Just when she'd settled down on the beach or in the tub, she'd get an idea about a new way to program a computer or a new theory of artificial intelligence or a new way to engineer genes."

"Jeans? Pants?"

Sylvia had been watching the pencil as she talked. Now she stopped moving it and looked at me with surprise. "Are you serious?" she said.

"I can be, if you want."

My answer seemed to confuse her. She picked up the pencil, shook it at me, and said, "You're a funny guy, Marlowe."

"Laugh a minute. So, she had these ideas."

Sylvia narrowed her eyes at me. "You never heard of genes? As in chromosomes?"

"It's not a hot topic where I come from."

"But still—" She stopped herself and asked the sixty-four-dollar question. "Where exactly *do* you come from?"

"I could tell you Bay City, like I tell everybody else."

"You could."

"Yeah. And you'd buy it because you're not a robot. You have social grace and the human touch."

"I'd *tell* you I bought it, anyway."

That went by like fog over water. I took a deep breath and said, "So, she had these ideas."

Sylvia shrugged and said, "Yes. And she had to go home and work them out."

"She had to?"

"They wouldn't leave her alone. She had to scratch the itch."

"You seem to have spent a lot of time inside Heavenly's head."

"We were friends."

Quickly, I said, "Where do you think she is?"

Sylvia thought about that. She considered it. She turned it over in her mind like a fine piece of sculpture. She said, "I don't know."

"Thoughts? Guesses? Conjectures?"

"I haven't seen her in a few days. Money like hers can buy a lot of travel."

"Her father wouldn't even guess *that* much."

"He's a little insecure. At the best of times they were not close. He wanted her to be a mechanical engineer. Her main interest is in genetic manipulation. Genes," she said carefully, "as in chromosomes. Not as in pants."

Leaping at that was pointless, so I said, "Maybe she's off scratching her itch."

"Maybe. If she is, you'll never find her."

"I found the house."

"Heavenly is not a house."

"No. But she has friends. Habits."

"Yes." Her eyes got dreamy. Right then, she was off with Heavenly. Suddenly, she snapped out of it and looked at me as if I'd just arrived. "Would you like to tour the grounds? I'll show you Heavenly's zoo," she said.

"Show me everything," I said.

* * *

We stepped out a back door and down two cement steps and were instantly joined by a small pot-metal robot dressed in the uniform of SSR security. As we walked along a path of yellow earth, he toddled a little behind us.

I said, "I think I almost met some of his brothers out in front."

"I'm not surprised. There are guards everywhere."

I glanced over my shoulder and said, "He doesn't look very bright."

"He doesn't have to be. If he knows you, he guards you. If he doesn't know you, he shoots."

"To kill or to injure?"

"Generally, to injure. But mistakes happen."

"I'm glad I'm not your mailman."

The backyard seemed to cover several counties. It contained a number of long brick buildings separated from each other by formal gardens. I could smell the flowers and hear water gently tinkling in fountains. It was a relaxing place. I wanted to relax. I couldn't relax. In the tower at the corner of the main house, I saw movement. I said, "What is Mr. Daise afraid of?"

"He has a list of things. But mostly he's afraid of industrial spies. People who want to know what he knows and won't stop at anything to find out."

"Is he right about these people?"

"Who knows? The world is full of industrial spies."

"And fear is real, even if you only imagine you're afraid. Maybe it's not just his imagination."

"What do you mean?"

"I mean that industrial spies who didn't know Mr.

Daise very well might think that trading Heavenly for a secret or two was a good idea."

She stopped walking and looked at me through narrow eyes. Sunlight glinted off them, made them look like diamond chips. "That's a nasty idea."

"So far it's *just* a nasty idea."

She nodded and pushed through a revolving door into the first building. Once through the door we were standing on a wide ledge overlooking a complicated and convincing seashore. Gulls wheeled in a painted sky over water that washed in waves over rocks and then receded. I couldn't see where the water receded to. Hard-looking green moss covered the rugged rocks where crabs no bigger than my fist marched carefully, as if stepping over bodies. In the pools between the rocks colorful tentacles swayed. The place even smelled like the ocean.

"I'm impressed," I said.

"Tidal pools are Mr. Daise's hobby."

"More than a hobby. What do you know about a room at the SSR building where Mr. Daise hides in the dark behind a pane of what is very probably bulletproof glass?"

"Not much. He interviewed me there a few times before he hired me."

The gulls, suspended on updrafts, flew down to have a look at us. They cried insults and floated back to the ceiling, where they wheeled again.

I said, "When's the last time you actually saw Mr. Daise?"

Sylvia bit her lip but continued to watch the birds. After a long time, she said, "It's been at least a month. I could check in my diary."

"Is it unusual for him to be out of sight for so long?"

"Not very. Mr. Daise has an apartment at the SSR building, and he is not much of a party animal. Nothing could have happened to him. You just talked to him this morning."

"I talked to a voice behind a dark piece of glass. You or the robotler were told about me by a voice over the phone."

"Meaning what?"

"Meaning somebody may be collecting people named Daise."

"If that's the case, Mr. Marlowe, I hope you're a very good detective." Before waiting for an answer, she turned suddenly and put her hand on the revolving door. "Come on. I'll show you Heavenly's zoo, if you still want to see it."

CHAPTER 12
The Money in Sagging Flesh

Sylvia Woods marched to the next building, passing roses and fountains as if they were just flowers and water. I followed, hurrying to catch up with the swaying butt and the pistoning arms. The cozy atmosphere was gone. I was a guy with nasty ideas, and that made me a nasty guy.

So far I had nothing much to chew on. If I went back to Malibu now, I'd stay there watching TV and inhaling strange smoke. Sylvia had to know more than she was telling. If she didn't, or she would not tell me, I would not only have to be a great detective, I would have to be a magician. I was neither.

I caught up with Sylvia and said, "Look, *I* didn't kidnap them." I had to jog to keep up with her.

She didn't look at me. "There hasn't been a ransom note. Maybe they weren't kidnapped." Her voice was hard as bathroom tile and just as cold.

"Maybe not," I said. "But wouldn't it be nice if we knew for sure?"

I was about three seconds behind her when she pushed through another revolving door. By the time I got into the building she looked like a different person, or anyway, like the person I'd been talking to in the library. She was facing me and smiling shyly as if she were about to ask me to dance. "You're right, Zoot. I guess I'm just a little upset." Her voice echoed while she pushed her glasses up her nose.

I said, "Don't feel like the Lone Ranger," but I was looking at the room we were standing in. I couldn't help myself. It was an unusual room.

It was a lot bigger than it looked from the outside, and the outside looked enormous. Down the center of the room, row on row of laboratory tables and equipment stretched to the far end. On the tables were enamel pans and shiny tools delicate enough to clean under a flea's fingernails. One of the tables had a lot of flasks and beakers connected by twisted glass tubes.

The equipment between the tables was big and many-piped. A heat dissipator circled the thick round body of each piece, its mirror surface reflecting me in a way that did not improve my looks. At the foot of each were a computer terminal and a chair made of black leather and chrome. Along the walls were aquarium tanks, each bubbling merrily. On shelves over them were hundreds of cages, stacked like high-rise apartments nearly to the ceiling. Some kind of metal scaffolding was built against the cages.

There were fish in the tanks and animals in the cages. Sylvia and I didn't concern the fish, but the animals began to move around and make noise. Some of them pawed the bars of their cages while they yipped pleadingly. They all looked at us with big haunted eyes.

The animals filled the room with a terrible smell. It had a solid presence, like a big animal itself, one that could not be ignored. It had all the worst features of every bad smell I had met on Earth. Next to it, cigarette smoke was a spring morning. Burning week-old grease was a day in the country. You could send that smell out to the cleaners but when you got it back it would smell just the same.

"Some zoo," I said. "What goes on here?"

"This is where Heavenly did her experiments."

"For instance?"

"Are you sure you want to know?"

I wasn't. I said, "Yes."

She put a finger to a cheek and crinkled her eyes as she walked across the dull black floor. I followed her with my eyes. This room was a lot nastier than any thought I'd had to date. She rode a metal frame along the scaffolding to a particular place on the wall, and then the frame traveled up the scaffolding like an elevator with her inside it.

Dogs, cats, and birds ran around inside their cages in circles, then looked through their bars and called out to her. A monkey put out his hand and was actually close enough to touch her with one finger. She shrank back, hurriedly found the cage she was looking for, and rode the frame back to the floor. She lugged the cage back to the laboratory table nearest me.

"Here's one you'll like," Sylvia said.

A dog stood in the center of the cage wagging its tail and barking at us. Each bark had a little cry at the end.

I said, "It's just a dog."

"Silly you," Sylvia said. "It used to be a cat."

"Huh?" She had surprised me. That grunt was the best I could do.

"Huh, yourself. It used to be a cat. Heavenly genetically altered it to make it a dog."

I whistled low through my teeth.

"I also have an archaeopteryx that used to be a parakeet."

"I can only assume that an archaeopteryx and a parakeet are not the same thing."

"Not hardly."

She showed me the archaeopteryx—a big winged thing that was as much lizard as bird. After that she showed me another dog—this one living in drifts of its own dandruff—a macaw with a bobbed beak, and a pigeon with a great set of boobs. *Sylvia* said they were great boobs. I had no opinion. Females on T'toom don't have them.

"What, exactly, was Heavenly trying to prove here?"

"I told you. She was into genetic manipulation. Among other things, she wanted to cure a lot of common complaints—dandruff, acne, warts, sagging flesh."

"Any money in sagging flesh?"

"Yes, but that wouldn't matter to Heavenly. She was—is—a humanitarian."

"All right. Say she is. How was she doing?"

"I don't know. I'm her social secretary, not her lab assistant."

"I said all right. I'm sorry I took a poke at her. She doesn't care a thing about money. Could anybody else make sense of this stuff?" I nodded at the laboratory.

Sylvia sighed. She was tired of fighting me. "I don't think so. I guess she kept notes, but I don't know where they'd be."

"Heavenly could be a big help finding them."

"Nasty," Sylvia said.

I nodded. We went back outside, and I breathed deeply. As we strolled along a gravel path in one of the formal gardens, I said, "Who takes care of these animals?"

Together, we said, "Robots."

I nodded and said, "I'll bet the noses on their faces are just for show."

Not long after that we were sitting on a cold stone bench watching water tumble down cement seashells of increasing size into a tub big enough for Whipper Will and all his friends to surf in. The sun was going down through the trees. Birds were singing. Flashy flowers pe   ed the air. All was right with the world except at le st one person was missing, maybe two, and my friends were short some surf-bots. Not too bad for this evil old world, but bad enough. I was thinking alternately about where I might go next and about how cold the bench was.

Sylvia adjusted her glasses and said, "I've been thinking."

"Novelty night."

"Are you always that clever after a hard day's detecting?"

"Sorry. Reflex. You've been thinking."

"I've been thinking. I don't know where Heavenly went, but I know her hangs. Maybe one of her friends will know where she went. Maybe she'll show up herself."

I shook my head and grumbled, "English."

"What?"

"Nothing. Let's go."

The garage was a big empty barn. I think bats lived

in the rafters. Maybe a bum lived in one of the corners. He was safe unless somebody mounted a major expedition. The only car parked on the vast expanse of oil-dotted concrete was a small blue boxy job that Sylvia unlocked and let me into.

She pushed a button on the dash, and the garage door opened. I looked back as we drove out Franklin and saw that the door was closing again all on its own.

I said, "Who owns the car parked in front?"

"It's one of Heavenly's. A present from her father. But she never drove it much. She preferred a Porsche she bought herself."

"Herself?"

"With the allowance Mr. Daise gave her. Do these questions mean anything?"

"Probably not. Not right now, anyway."

My guts were trying to tell me something. And not just that they hadn't particularly enjoyed lunch. I simmered for a few seconds and turned to look behind us again. There was a car back there. It was an off-green car that was new about the time Philip Marlowe took his first case. "Slow down," I said.

"Backseat driver?"

"What? Slow down. I think somebody's following us, and I want to get a look at them."

Sylvia nodded, and she turned right at a little residential street that jutted at an angle to La Brea. The car rolled slowly along as if Sylvia and I were looking for an address. I glanced over my shoulder and saw that the off-green car had just turned the corner and was trundling about a half block behind us.

"Stop the car."

We double-parked almost at the next corner. The slow-moving car waited behind us for a second or two,

then, not to be conspicuous, it drifted around us like
a leaf around a rock in a stream. Sylvia and I both got
a good look at who was in the car following us. Three
gorillas in suits.

I said, "You ever see them before?"

"Who knows? All gorillas look alike to me."

"Sure. But three gorillas driving a car and wearing
suits? I think those are the same three I played patty-
cake with this morning at the SSR building." I pretended to think for a moment, but nothing useful
bubbled to the surface. I said, "Let's get going. They'll
come around again in a minute."

Sylvia turned a couple of corners, and we were
back on La Brea, heading south past gaudy little joints
selling anything you could ever want. But if you were
smart, you wouldn't want to get it in any of those
places. Traffic was heavy, and there was not much
room to maneuver. Neither of us spoke. I couldn't help
checking behind us now and then, and finally the sore
neck I was getting paid off.

"There they are," I said.

Sylvia shook her head at the going-home commute
traffic that surrounded us. She said, "And us with no
place to go."

CHAPTER 13
Hangs

By sweating a little and getting horns blown at it, the off-green car squeezed closer to us. By the time we got to Beverly, it was two cars behind us, where it seemed as comfortable as a babe in a cradle.

The light was green, but we waited for three cars to finish making illegal left turns before we rolled forward at a hesitant clip only slightly faster than I can walk. Our tail stayed two cars behind us.

Nervously, Sylvia said, "We could stop and see what they want."

"We could dance the tarantella on the roof of their car too. It would tell us as much. If they wanted to talk, they wouldn't have gone around us up in Hollywood."

"What then?" The worry in her eyes was not there because of the traffic.

"They're just following us to see where we go. Make it difficult."

"Make it—" Sylvia stopped talking suddenly. "OK." She hunched over the wheel, full of resolve.

Sylvia didn't break any traffic laws, but she also didn't make any friends as she got over to the right-hand lane and went west on Third to a cross street that was called Martel on one side of the thoroughfare and Hauser on the other.

"Los Angeles streets," I said and shook my head.

"A little game for the relatives visiting from back east." Sylvia turned the car onto Hauser. It was a broad street lined with identical tall white buildings, each with a small fringe of lawn around it and lots of parking spaces. The street doglegged, and smaller streets branched off to the side. The tall white buildings surrounded us like the walls of a maze. The off-green car turned onto Hauser.

Sylvia turned up one of the smaller streets, and I could see that it branched again further on. I was lost already. "What kind of a place is this?" I said.

"La Brea Towers," she said without looking at me. "People get lost in here all the time." She turned right at a traffic circle, went around two streets, and up the third.

"Unusual way to get tenants. I don't see the gorillas."

Sylvia turned again, and we circled one of the big buildings. A cream-colored Cadillac was letting a spry white-haired woman off under a long green awning. We kept circling and found our way to Fairfax, where we stopped for a red light. I looked across the asphalt playing field of a school on the corner and saw the green car, or one like it, nosing out between two of the apartment buildings.

"Hit it," I said.

Sylvia turned right, causing a car going northbound on Fairfax to skid and honk at us as it stopped too quickly. "I hate people who drive like idiots," she said, "especially when they're me."

We made our way through darkening side streets, where in nice houses people were getting ready for dinner in rooms full of homey yellow light. At Olympic, Sylvia sighed and turned west. "How was that?" she said.

"Pretty slick," I said. "I hope those gorillas are as lost as I am."

We played stop-and-go all down Olympic until Sylvia turned into a crowded parking structure behind an enclosed mall big enough to be the packing crate for a small city. People were still going home, not shopping, and we found a parking place pretty quick. After Sylvia turned off the engine we sat watching cars circle through the dim cement cavern looking for that perfect parking spot. I could hear Sylvia breathing. I could smell her, too. She smelled good. I was back in the Daise formal garden.

We rested until Sylvia said, "Well?"

"Well, Heavenly didn't hang in the parking lot, did she?"

Sylvia almost laughed. We left the car and walked through the parking structure to the mall, gathering glances from curious shoppers. Cars roared in the enclosed space like rolling thunder. A green car full of gorillas would be nothing special. It would sound like that too.

The mall in Malibu would have been a wart on the neck of the one we were walking through now. The place was at least five stories high and disappeared into the misty distance. I wouldn't have been able to see the far end anyway because of the cute sculptures sprawling down the center of the promenade. I wondered if the place had its own weather.

Fairy music that came from everywhere and no-where floated on the air with the smells of popcorn and Mexican food and new shoe leather. It made a heady mix with the vague echoes of moving, talking shoppers.

"Why is everything air-conditioned within an inch of its life?" I said. My nose was numbing up again.

"It's kind of a status thing."

"I get it. The colder you are, the more money you have." A bull of a man in a ridiculous red uniform was watching us from his station in front of a bank of private elevators. As we walked on, I said, "People live here?"

"Live and work both."

"Is there an undertaker?"

"No."

"I wouldn't think so. It wouldn't fit the mood. Not unless he could have tiny white lights blinking in his window and he could sell popcorn on the side. Too bad, though. An undertaker in the mall would be a great selling point. You'd *never* have to go out-side."

We went up a flight in a glass elevator inside a clock that showed its gears working and walked down to a bookstore called Nurture/Nature. The front of the store was paneled in rustic wood. We entered through a wide doorway over which two very com-plicated and artistic Ns were burned, intertwining, into the wood.

Inside, the bookstore continued the outdoorsy theme. It busted a gut trying to look as if the entire inside were outside. Bookshelves seemed hewn from fallen trees. The ceiling was painted a cloud-flecked blue. Autumn leaves and pine needles were painted on the brown floor. Guitar music played softly but persistently against the aggressively jaunty music that managed to get in through the open door. Whoever owned the shop had missed out making the place smell like pine needles, but nobody's perfect.

Only the customers didn't fit. From the looks of the earnest crowd, they had only a nodding acquaintance with roughing it, and the lack of experience had taken on a sort of romantic glow. They were casually well-dressed but not very rugged.

"I should have worn my cowboy hat," I said.

"It's true," said Sylvia, "they're a little heavy on decor, but otherwise, it's a good bookstore. They have an enormous selection of books on genetics and tanning."

"Together or individually?"

"Both. You'd be amazed at how many people are interested in both subjects."

"Probably. This is one of Heavenly's hangs?"

Sylvia nodded. "Her favorite bookstore."

We wandered for a while, watching faces and catching patches of conversation. None of it meant much to me. After we'd cased the whole store, Sylvia and I walked down an aisle lined with big books with colorful covers showing balls with spikes and short twisty trains. Just about every book had the word "virus" in the title. At the moment, nobody was in the aisle. Sylvia picked up a book just to have something in her hands and said, "I didn't see anybody I know." She sounded disappointed.

"You said there are a lot of people interested in this stuff. Not all of them would know Heavenly. And you wouldn't know all of them that she knew."

"Yeah. I'm a hell of a social secretary."

"We're not dead yet. Let's talk to the guy behind the counter."

Sylvia followed me back to the front of the store. I had to stand back from the counter to see over it. On top of the counter was a cardboard display rack filled with copies of a book called *Tanning is in Your Blood* by Genetics MacDonald. First Time in Paperback! a headline screamed in red. The cover featured a good-looking woman wearing a bathing suit only a little more revealing than the one Heavenly had been wearing in her photograph. She was as brown as a Christmas turkey and reclining on a rock whose rough texture made a nice contrast with her smooth skin. The whole thing was pretty artistic. A human male might buy the book just to get the cover.

A thin blond man with the ghost of a mustache stopped reading a book, closed it on his finger, and looked down at me. Long straight hair hung like a curtain over one eye, and a well-broken-in low-grade smile glowed on his face like a friendly fire. He wore a brown sweater with silhouettes of reindeer on it, and a big watch with a golden worm holding it on his wrist.

"Was there something?" he said. Then Sylvia walked up, and he lost all interest in me. The low-grade smile became a barn-burner, and he almost jumped over the counter at her. He began to babble, "Heavenly, darling, I haven't seen you in here in ages! Where *have* you been keeping yourself? Did you know that Puffy Tootsweet is having a party at her beach house tonight? She told me to pass the word, but I never thought. . . ." Evidently the thought that he might be passing the word to Heavenly was just too much for him. He reached for his chest to grab his breath, giving Sylvia a chance to say, "I'm not Heavenly."

"Not?"

"Heavenly. I'm Sylvia Woods, her social secretary."

"Well, where has she been keeping herself?"

I dropped my dime by saying, "We were hoping that you had some ideas about that."

"Me?" The smile was turned down a notch, set on good fellowship rather than on stun.

Sylvia introduced us, and the clerk reached over the counter to shake my hand. "Private detective, eh? Trouble is your business? *The Maltese Falcon?* All that sort of thing?" He was delighted at some private joke.

"Maltese falcon?" I said.

The clerk, Sylvia, and another customer reacted to my question with the astonishment usually reserved for my nose. The clerk ran from his perch behind the counter and returned in seconds with a slim black volume bearing a photo of a stylized statue of a bird on its cover—*The Maltese Falcon* by Dashiell Hammett. I promised that I would read it as soon as I had the time, thus preventing the clerk, Sylvia, and the customer from jumping down my throat.

While the clerk was ringing up *The Maltese Falcon*, he said, "Why would you think that I knew where Heavenly was?" A horrifying idea struck him. He froze and with eyebrows raised looked at me. "She's not missing, is she?"

"She hasn't been in here for a while, has she?"

"Well, no."

We both waited while his inquisitive glance struck me and slid off. I became aware of a fast-picking down-home number dropping through the suddenly still air from speakers in the ceiling. If I had confused him, that was just as well. Daise family business was none of his. I could see him wondering if it was worth his trouble and maybe the goodwill of a customer to ask too many questions. The good sense of a shopkeeper won out, and he gaily bid us goodbye as we left the store. "See you at Puffy's," he called after us.

We strolled through the mall, just a couple of crazy kids without enough to do. Sylvia said, "Heavenly loved Puffy's parties. She might show up for it."

"If she knew Puffy was throwing a party."

"That clerk in there is not the only person Puffy told to spread the word."

"No. He wouldn't be. All right. Where does this Puffy live?" I was aware of a dull gamy smell in the air. While Sylvia answered my question, I discovered where the smell was coming from. Three gorillas in suits. They had seen us too. They were moving quickly down the other side of the mall toward the walkway, where they could cross over to us.

Still answering my question, Sylvia said, "Puffy lives down at the beach in Malibu."

"Let's go."

She laughed that Mozart laugh of hers. "I can't go like this. If you don't dress up for one of Puffy's parties, you're not dressed at all."

"Come on," I said and grabbed her arm. I pulled her toward Cuthbertson's, the big department store at the nearest end of the mall.

"What's going on?"

"Evidently our friends were *not* as lost as I was."

Sylvia looked where I was looking, and her face went slack. We moved along together, not quite running. She didn't need to be dragged.

We walked in through the perfume department and kept going. I said, "Keep moving. Take the long way back to the car and wait for me." She nodded, touched the bridge of her glasses, and went.

I turned around and walked back the way we had come. The gorillas had just entered the store and were standing in the wide doorway trying to guess which direction we'd gone. They looked as confused as cats in a tree. Tiger, the half-bright one, picked up a Taj Mahal bottle and wrinkled his nose at the contents. Spike slapped his hand, and he put it down.

I came around the corner on the far side of the gleaming counter and stood behind them for a moment before I said, "Looking for something that smells like a banana?"

They whirled on me with their hands halfway into their coats but relaxed when they saw I had my hands in my pockets. The only thing I packed was a water pistol, but the gorillas didn't know that. Spike said, "We don't need the heat."

"Says you. Let's go for a little walk."

"Jake with us," Spike said. He and I walked together. The other two gorillas were not far behind.

The tinkly music and plastic charm of the mall retreated to another world. The gorillas and I could have been walking along a deserted road in the middle of nowhere. But we weren't. We were walking through a mall toward the Nurture/Nature Bookstore. I kept my hands in my pockets and waited for Spike to make the first move. It would be interesting to see what it would be.

At last Spike said, "Where's Heavenly Daise?"

I tried to keep the surprise out of my voice. "That seems to be a popular question."

"Yeah?" The word hung in the air, quickly growing brown and brittle. "And what's the popular answer?"

"Tell me why I should know."

"You're looking for her, ain't you?"

"Says who?"

Behind us, Duke grunted. Tiger wasn't paying any attention. He was looking into the big pretty windows.

"Says us," said Spike. He opened his coat a little to show me the pistol hanging inside. "Let's see yours."

We walked a few more steps, and I ducked into the Nurture/Nature Bookstore. The three gorillas were right behind me, of course. They were just in time to hear me shout, "You're in luck, folks! Here's Genetics MacDonald, himself!"

The clerk looked in my direction, his eyes wide, while customers flowed in from the rest of the store. I ran down a side aisle against the tide—sometimes being small can have its advantages—and through a stockroom at the back of the store. I could hear shouting coming from up front. It could have meant anything.

I hurried quickly among the crowded bookshelves and cardboard boxes. "Wait a minute," a fat, honey-haired girl with glasses cried. But by that time I was out the back door and moving fast along a narrow cement service corridor. Not many doors away I found a freight elevator, which I took down to the loading dock. From there, I walked quickly around to the customer side of the mall and found Sylvia's car. She was in it, under the wheel, huddling with herself, though the evening was not cold.

I knocked on the window, and she jumped. When she saw it was me, she unlocked the passenger door, and I slid in beside her. While I caught my breath, she said, "What did they want?"

"What do we all want? Heavenly Daise."

Sylvia nodded a tiny nod.

"That mean something to you?"

"No," Sylvia said as if it could mean yes. "I'd just hate to think of those gorillas finding her before we do."

"They don't act like gorillas. How might they be connected with Heavenly?"

"I don't know. They're not her type."

"No. Not the type of anybody who's nice. Yet they knew Heavenly was missing and that I was looking for her. That means they've either been talking to her father or someone close to her father."

"Who?"

"If I knew that, I'd be a lot less confused than I am right now. Start the car. We're going to Puffy's party."

CHAPTER 14

No White Tie, No Tails

While Sylvia drove us back to the Daise place, she explained again why she couldn't go to one of Puffy's parties dressed the way she was. The fact that being in Santa Monica she was three-quarters of the way to Malibu didn't seem to make any difference. Nothing would satisfy her but that she must go home and change. It made as much sense to me as a Gino and Darlene movie. I gave her Whipper Will's address. When she stopped by later in her splendid party clothes, I would drive her to Puffy's house in the old Chevy.

"That's OK, I guess. Classic cars are in."

"In what?"

Sylvia laughed, but didn't explain. I was witty, all right. Yes, I was.

Traffic was still heavy, and it took us almost an hour to get back to the Daise mansion. Sylvia left me in front and parked her car in the garage. It opened magically when she was half a block away and then closed behind her.

I sat in my car for a while, watching the ripening sun carefully climb down through the branches of trees toward the foothills. Meanwhile, people were getting home, putting their cars away, emptying the streets. Or maybe that was wishful thinking. I was doing a lot of that lately. For instance, I was wishfully thinking that I might make sense out of this case.

Somebody, maybe Gotterdammerung, had destroyed the surfers' surf-bots so that Gotterdammerung could win the yoyogurt recipe. That would have been a dirty enough business, but there was more. Surfing Samurai Robots, the biggest name in robots, had bought up everything that had anything to do with surf-bots, seemingly so that the broken robots could not be fixed or replaced. Unless SSR was working for Gotterdammerung—which was as likely as Sylvia going to Puffy's party in her jeans—I could not see any motive for SSR to care who won the Surf-O-Rama. Maybe they had suddenly taken a big interest in yoyogurt. I shook my head. I might as well try to build the Parthenon from a pile of rocks.

Meanwhile, I had been hired to find the supposedly runaway daughter of the owner of SSR. Not only was her father looking for her, but so were three gorillas who seemed awfully well connected.

Was the fact that SSR stood out from this mess like a rubber duck in a punch bowl just an odd coincidence, no more meaningful than a cloud looking like a slaberingeo, or did SSR have its fingers in more pies than any multinational corporation had any right to? I don't believe in coincidences. It isn't healthy.

The sun was an orange hump above the black foothills now, and the mellow air had a bracing cold edge to it. In the sky, a good-looking sunset was playing. A charmer. But it didn't tell me why this odd coincidence involving SSR.

I started the car and drove home. The traffic was heavy at first, but by the time I got to Malibu, it had thinned to the point that I could turn left into the garage without having to wait half an hour.

The gang was in the kitchen climbing over each other to reach slices from a steaming wheel of pizza. The commotion stopped when I came in, then started again almost immediately. Everybody wanted to know if I'd found out who-dun-it to their surf-bots. Whipper Will didn't say anything. He just sat in the corner with his arm dangling across Bingo's shoulder, watching the show through an unreadable expression.

"No," I said, "but it's early yet. I'm going to a party this evening."

Captain Hook said, "Pretty aggro, dude, considering what we're paying you."

"Considering what you're paying me, I've been on the case all day, and I'll probably be on it at that party." My tone was not pretty. I was tired and hungry for something other than grease, and I needed a bath. I almost snarled.

"No offense, dude," said Thumper as he expertly folded the angle of the pizza slice back with his tongue and shoved half of the rolled-over part into his mouth. Around his chewing, he said, "Whose party?"

"Puffy Tootsweet."

"Bitchen!" they all intoned. Captain Hook said, "I'm about stoked for a Puffy Tootsweet party."

"You been stoked for years," Bingo said. Everybody laughed. Even Captain Hook didn't lose his smile.

"Sorry. This is business."

They stopped laughing and looked at me as if I'd just swallowed the Pacific Ocean whole. Captain Hook said, "Oh, sure. Well, who's your client, hot dog? Get us into the party or we'll fire you."

I shook my head. "You can fire me if you want to. I only wish you'd done it sooner. If you just wanted invitations to parties, it would have saved me a lot of grief. But I thought you wanted a little detecting done."

Whipper Will came through the kitchen door carrying a big blue ceramic bowl in both hands. I hadn't even seen him leave the room. He said, "Who's for yoyogurt?"

"We're discussing a little something here," Captain Hook said.

"It's a new flavor," Whipper Will said.

"So?" said Captain Hook. "We're talking about a Puffy Tootsweet bash here."

Before he finished his sentence, Thumper said, "What flavor?"

Offhandedly, as if he said it every day, Whipper Will said, "Alfalfa sprout."

"Cowabunga!" Mustard cried. There was a scattering of "Ahh-rooh!"s from around the room. Mustard took the bowl and put it next to the pizza. Mopsie (or was it Flopsie?) threw a handful of teaspoons on the table with a clatter. The surfers dug in. Occasionally, one of them managed to squeeze out a "bitchen" between the lip-smacking.

Meanwhile, Captain Hook glared at Whipper Will with the jeweled eyes of an angry god. He said, "Mighty cool, ain't you, dude?"

Captain Hook's glare was so much smoke to Whipper Will. He lounged against the doorway, relaxed as a python after dinner. "Zoot is doing his work. Let him."

"The big kahuna," Captain Hook said as if the words were poison. "Big fuckin' kahuna."

"Look," I said, "you can crash the party if you want. Hell, you can come with me. But it won't help me find out who diddled with your surf-bots if everybody knows who I'm working for."

Captain Hook's eyes lost their luster. He turned suddenly and went out, slamming the back door behind him. Thumper looked up, saw nothing that interested him, and went back to exclaiming over the bowl of alfalfa sprout yoyogurt.

I said, "I'm going to take a shower. After that, I'll need some clothes." Whipper Will nodded.

The hot water felt good. I wrapped a towel around my middle and went to Whipper Will's room. He sat on the floor with a big pile of clothes on one side and a much smaller pile on the other. Invisible clouds of human musk weighed down the air in the room like a tent. Whipper Will took garment after garment from the small pile, held it up to the appropriate part of my body, and threw it aside.

Then, we started getting lucky. In twenty minutes I was wearing a lime green coat, a beet purple shirt, and shocking blue pants that on Whipper Will were walking shorts. They matched the blue gloves. A wide-brimmed hat rested lightly on my nose. I looked like what's left after Dollar Day is over, but Whipper Will assured me that nobody would notice. They also wouldn't notice that nothing quite fit. The baggy look was in style. I still felt more comfortable in my brown suit.

By that time, the surfers were in the living room zoned out on yoyogurt. On the television, a gigantic creature stomped through a city breathing flame. I didn't want to know if the broadcast was news or entertainment.

All the yoyogurt was gone, but a lot of pizza was left. As I ate, I watched Captain Hook through the window. Just outside the fringe of light thrown from the kitchen, he stood stiffly with his hands in his pockets, looking out at the ocean. I didn't know for sure that his thoughts were as dark as the water, but it was the way to bet.

I sat around over an hour, watching Godzilla turn Tokyo into kindling over and over again. The movie was on videotape, the surfers could see the destruction as often as they liked. Me, it was putting to sleep.

Then the doorbell rang, and I was off the floor and down the hall before Godzilla had a chance to stomp out so much as another cigarette butt. I opened the door on a person compared to whom the Sylvia Woods I had seen that afternoon was only a pale imitation.

She was wearing a top that shone like metal, moved like cloth, but looked as if it had been poured onto her. Every curve was in sight and gleamed like the highlights on a new car. Wrapped around her hips was a skirt in a gaudy print showing red birds and blue flowers and some very jagged green palm fronds. I had seen bigger washcloths. Her hair fell to her shoulders in tight red curls. She still had the same face, but deftly applied makeup made every feature more so. The one clinker was the glasses, but they didn't clink much.

While I was taking all this in, she was going over me the way a jeweler might look for a rhinestone in a diamond ring. She smiled while she did it, which made it all right. We left Sylvia's car in the tiny parking lot in front of the house, and I drove her and the Chevrolet deeper into Malibu.

It was a beautiful night. The air was cooler than it had been during the day, but it was the soft coolness of a silk scarf that had been wrapped around a cold champagne bottle. The brisk traffic was ghostly despite the constant thrum of engines. You could pretend the engines were just the wind.

Far out, a couple of lights flashed on a small boat. Looking across the curve of coastline, I could see lights strung out like a necklace against the black water. Inside it, moving headlights weaseled around curves.

We passed beyond the clutch of small stores and restaurants called downtown Malibu, and darkness closed in around us. High on a hill, a floodlit castle built by a doctor with too much money stood out against the night like a pasteboard cutout.

My headlights swept along the road, carving a tunnel through the engulfing darkness. Though I could not see them, I could still feel a cliff rising to one side, and the openness of the ocean on the other. A pungent smell of low tide blew in through the whistling crack at the top of my window.

"Turn left here," Sylvia said. It was the first time either of us had spoken since we'd left the house.

I waited for traffic to pass, then turned in to a private road that led down to a parking lot. A young man in a short red coat and white pants ran out of the darkness and up to the car. He opened the door for Sylvia. Then, without waiting for her to get out, he ran to my side, opened the door, and held it open. "Good evening, sir," he said in a peremptory way in a heavily accented voice. He looked back along the road. I did the same, and I could see that I was holding up the parade. There were three cars behind me now and another one turning in off PCH. As I got out of the car, the parking attendant shoved a claim check into my hand.

Before I'd walked three steps the tires of my car squealed as the young man broke several traffic laws racing my car around the corner into the lot. Sylvia joined me. As we followed the crowd out onto a pier rimmed with Christmas lights, I said, "Puffy lives off-shore?"

"Not as such."

I raised my hat so that I could look at her more carefully. Her lips were pressed tightly together, try-ing not to smile. Sylvia pointed out at the water just off the pier. A moment later, a bug-eyed sea monster rose from the ocean, sluicing water down its smooth sides.

CHAPTER 15
Hard Work

A few people in the crowd laughed as if this were all good clean fun. More of them, like me, just looked worried—smiling like good sports about to undergo a quiz show prank while we wondered if the indignity would be worth the trouble.

What had risen from the water wasn't a sea monster, of course, but a diving bell with thick glass portholes. A door swung open and clanged against the side. A man dressed in a dark uniform but for his glowing white shoes and white peaked cap threw across a tiny bridge that clamped to the edge of the pier. He invited us to cross over.

Like a trained pig, I trotted across with the others and stepped over the coaming. The man in the uniform glanced at me, glanced again, and seemed about to make a comment. Instead, he looked away and said, "Step lively, folks. The fun's already begun."

The inside of the diving bell was lined with a thick shag carpet that was blue in the blue lights that glowed gently between the portholes. The place was damp and smelled as if it had never been dry. We sat with our backs against a raised lip that ran under the portholes and our feet toward a transparent pillar enclosing water that stood about halfway to the ceiling.

The captain called, "Don't get too comfy, folks. It'll all be over in a minute." He laughed as he shut the door and dogged it down with a spoked wheel, then walked to one side of the compartment, where he grabbed a big lever.

"I want a drink," a big man in a suit and tie said as if he were demanding liberty and justice for all. The pudgy woman next to him tried to shush him, but he wouldn't be shushed. "I'm thirsty."

"No drinking in the bell, sir." The captain threw the lever, and water bubbled up in the central pillar. I was chilled by the sensation that we were dropping rapidly through the cold black water, though I'm sure the temperature of the air in the bell didn't change. We all looked like frozen corpses in the blue light. No one said anything, but looked around. If they were like me, they were watching for the first sign of leakage.

The water reached the top of the pillar and began to fall. The bell was rising now. I leaned across and whispered in Sylvia's ear, "It was a swell party. Thanks."

"You just wait," she said.

When the water was at the halfway mark again, the captain bounded across the bell and undogged the door. He flung it open and stood aside. "Last one out's a rotten egg," he said and laughed.

The diving bell was now docked at the edge of a big pool inside an enormous cavern. Waves slapped up and back. The place looked natural but may have been just as phony as the colored lights illuminating it from behind outcroppings.

Across a wide shelf of rock was the front of a house. Its smooth wall swelled from the rugged cavern wall as if the house had burst through from inside the rock but had been too big to escape. Laughter, talk, and loud music recommending that we "all go surfin' now!" because "everybody's learnin' how!" poured from an open door along with the smell of liquor and of the same strange smoke that my friends rejoiced in. Dim shadows moved behind the windows.

The thirsty man led our group across the shelf. His pudgy companion toddled after him, working hard to keep up. Couples clutched at each other and giggled as they shared private jokes that needed this particular moment to be funny. In our turn, Sylvia and I walked through the doorway and were hit with a wall of noise and smell nearly physical enough to lean on. I couldn't see much—nobody could in that confidential, suggestive light. It was so indirect, it seemed to be coming from another state.

A woman not much taller than I glided toward us with her arms outstretched. "Bro's!" she cried as if she had discovered us after a long search through dense jungle. A blue dress—blue seemed to be a popular color that year—that fell in a straight line from her broad shoulders to the floor covered her bulk. The dress wasn't just blue, of course. Macaws with their banana beaks intact cavorted across it. Hair of indeterminate color—at least in that light—was braided and wound around the top of the woman's head like a crown.

She took a hit from a small brown cigarette she pinched in one fleshy hand and cried out again. This time, she cried, "Heavenly!" We could barely hear her.

"Not Heavenly, Puffy," Sylvia shouted back. She

introduced herself like a quarterback shouting signals. My throat became raw just listening to her. At
that, I could barely hear what she said. Puffy must
have been a lip reader.

Puffy made a quick recovery. She said, "Radical,
surfer girl! Heavenly always wears her hair like that!
Always stoked about that hair!" She looked at me with
friendly curiosity and said, "And who is this?"

"Zoot Marlowe," Sylvia said, "meet the Empress of
'Bu, Puffy Tootsweet!"

"Radical," I said. I couldn't hear myself.

"Bitchen costume," she said and lost interest in
me. She invited Sylvia to have a brewski and circulate.
She nodded at me and cried, "Bro's!" as she greeted
the next couple to come through the door.

Sylvia took me back to a bathroom hung with nets,
spiny globular fish—now dead and stiff—and seashells. The fish had been rigged as lamps. The bathtub
was filled with ice and drinks and cups of what I suspected was yoyogurt. We selected cans of brewski,
popped our tops, and circulated out into a bedroom.
The bed was heaped with coats, and copies of some
slick publication called *Brown Genes Magazine* were
fanned across a dressing table. On the cover, a healthy
woman was surfing to shore, her open lab coat flap-
ping in the wind. One hand was raised and holding a
test tube.

"If Heavenly's anywhere tonight, she's here," Sylvia said.

"Sure. Be here or be skwere," I said, using a crowbar to force the words to rhyme. We shouted at each
other. I could see a long night of shouting ahead.

Sylvia nodded and glanced around. I doubted
Heavenly would be at the party. Not if she'd been ab-

ducted. Not if she wanted, for her own reasons, to stay missing. But somebody who knew her or knew about her might be there. Leads are everywhere if you keep an open mind. I wanted to tell Sylvia this, but right at the moment, it seemed to be a lot of work.

The thirsty guy in the suit no more belonged at that party than a polar bear belonged at a luau. However, I fit right in. Most of the guests wore the chino pants and boisterous T-shirts that my surfer friends wore all the time. But I was a really aggro dude, I can tell you. More than one dude or chick fingered my groovy threads and smiled with approval. My nose and height didn't seem to be an issue. They were, after all, part of a bitchen costume.

The house was a maze of rooms. It seemed designed to get lost in. Sylvia and I passed through a zone of loud music where dancers shook as if with some rare disease. "Two girls for every boy!" the recorded singers roared.

Right next door, guests who had all the energy of fallen trees watched scenes from *Endless Summer* on a big-screen TV. They couldn't listen to it because the music from the room next door threw itself desperately against the wall, causing the video room to vibrate like a bass drum. The more athletic of the people in the room lifted brewskis to their mouths or spooned yoyogurt.

Beyond that, we rounded a corner, and the music was suddenly far away. I banged the side of my head with my hand. "I've gone deaf," I said. My voice was lighter than feathers in the sudden void.

"No," said Sylvia. "It's the baffles. They keep the music from spreading to places you don't want it."

"I don't want it anywhere."

Sylvia opened her mouth to make a comment when something snagged her attention. "Look," she said.

She was pointing into the next room, where a big crowd was gathered around a golden robot crouched into the classic Quasimodo surfing position. Bitchen, I thought. A surf-bot, I thought. I was wrong, but just barely.

The big golden robot was part of a game called Slamma Jammer. A squat, solid guy with cannonball muscles was holding a small box that was nearly lost in his fist. With it, he controlled the actions of the robot, who danced and weaved on a surfboard attached to a set of pneumatic pistons. The board ripped through a convincing holographic pipeline synchronized with stereophonic ocean sounds. Spectators dodged realistic spray that disappeared at the limits of the projected image. If the robot wiped out, the big guy lost. The game looked like fun, but it was no more surfing than chess is war.

"Wipeout!" the crowd cried as the mechanical board flipped the robot into the air. In the air, the robot turned like a cat, landed lightly on his feet, and froze standing upright on the motionless surfboard. The big guy shook his head and smiled good-naturedly. A pretty girl, wearing a hot pink bikini that made Sylvia look overdressed, mussed the big guy's hair and led him away.

That evening, I talked to the big guy and as many other people as I could about the Slamma Jammer game. The big guy didn't know which end of a screwdriver to grab, and he was not alone. But anybody who claimed to know anything about surf-bots or robot holo-games told me that the Slamma Jammer robot

and surf-bots were different. You could not fix one
with parts from another. SSR wouldn't even dirty
their corporate hands manufacturing a surfing holo-
game.

Later, Sylvia and I were sitting on a couch in a
room where galaxies and amoebas of light floated
across the walls and ceiling. Slow, contemplative music no louder than birdsong droned from a pair of
speakers. It seemed about right for our mood. I felt as
if I'd just spent three hours rolling down a mountain
in a barrel. All for nothing. The whispers of convers-
ing couples hissed at us from a matching couch across
the way.

A woman wearing tight black pants and a T-shirt
with the legend OFFICIAL KANSAS CITY SURFING
TEAM walked in and stopped abruptly, probably
shocked by the lack of noise. She backed into a corner
and stood there, lost in the hypnotic light and the soft
music. A moment later she cried, "Heavenly" and
hunkered down next to us. She didn't wait for Sylvia
to respond, but balanced herself with a hand on Sylvia's knee and went on, "It's been so long since I've
seen you. I should have called, I know, but you
wouldn't believe how busy I am; with Arno sculpting
in iron these days, it seems we never get out of the
foundry." She yammered on, barely drawing breath.
In her own way, she was amazing.

After going on about Arno and the ironmongery
he was welding together, she said, "And I was wondering—" She sounded tentative, as if she were picking her way across a wet floor. "I was wondering if
you were done with this month's copy of *Brown Genes
Magazine*."

When the woman began, Sylvia had tried to slip in

a word of explanation. She might as well have tried to slip between two coats of paint. After a while Sylvia gave up and nodded politely to the woman's chatter. People had been mistaking Sylvia for Heavenly all evening. It didn't bother her, but she wanted to set the record straight. Setting the record straight the fifth or sixth time was boring.

The woman waited for a comment. Sylvia said, "I'm not Heavenly, Isadora. I'm her social secretary, Sylvia Woods." Sylvia's voice was tired, mechanical. It had been dredged up with difficulty from deep inside her. Being social all evening is hard work, even for a social secretary.

Isadora never missed a beat. She said, "Of course." Silly her. She looked at me. "And who is *this*?" she said with the predatory intonation of a chicken hawk asking about the chicken on the next roost.

"Zoot Marlowe," I said and stuck out my hand. She took it, held it briefly, as if it were made of bone china, and let go. She told me that she was charmed. Maybe she was. She looked at me while she spoke to Sylvia.

"I hate to be a bother," Isadora said, "but I can't afford *Brown Genes* myself. All my money goes for supplies for Arno's work."

Sylvia shook her head and said, "Art's a bitch, isn't it?"

Isadora snapped her head to look at Sylvia. Sylvia's expression was one of mild sympathy, as if Isadora had announced that she had a hangnail. Isadora erected a smile. It was OK for the moment but would not stand much strain.

Sylvia said, "Actually, this month's copy of *Brown Genes* never came."

"Ah," Isadora said, relieved by Sylvia's friendly, confidential admission.

"Which is odd. The subscription is not due to run out for months."

"Well," said Isadora, "if it ever shows up, you know where you can reach me." She handed over a card and stood up in one flowing motion. She told me again that I had charmed her and strolled out of the room.

I looked at the card in Sylvia's hand. It was shiny with some kind of metallic foil. Both Isadora's and Arno's names were engraved on it, and under that it said, in large letters drawn like girders, HEAVY METAL. I stood up and said, "I'll be back in a minute."

"Isadora turn you on?"

"In a manner of speaking."

My hearts racing each other, I walked from the room before Sylvia could make a clever comment on my sexuality.

I got lost only twice on my way back to the bedroom where the coats were piled on the bed. At the moment, two people were sprawled on top of the coats. The one on top with her legs spread looked like Isadora. The guy on the bottom, who was not fighting very hard to get free, may or may not have been Arno.

Ignoring them, I walked to the dressing table and flipped open the top copy of *Brown Genes*. In the dim, tasteful light I barely managed to read the tiny type on the first page. The main office of *Brown Genes Magazine* was in Huntington Beach.

I stood there pondering. The pair on the bed didn't mind. They were busy crushing coats and making the springs sing. Suddenly, they stopped and looked up. I looked up too. Somewhere in the house, somebody had just screamed in terror.

CHAPTER 16

Crashing, Bashing, Smashing

I ran in the direction of the sound and found a silent crowd at the front door looking out at the rock shelf. As I arrived, the loud music stopped in the middle of a word, leaving only the echo of powerful engines rumbling in the big cavern outside.

I glided through the crowd, trying not to get stepped on, and came to Puffy Tootsweet, who stood in the middle of the doorway frowning. She was not the bimbo she pretended to be. Standing in the doorway took a certain amount of grit. Rolling onto the rock shelf through a tunnel hidden behind a petrified curtain were the members of Gotterdammerung.

The gang pulled up smartly in a row in front of the house. They smiled and licked their lips and limbered up their leather-gloved hands. Without a word, they turned off their motorcycles and dismounted. Tankhauser swaggered toward the front door with his gang in tow. He would have walked in the front door, but Puffy did not get out of his way.

Tankhauser stood there casually. He didn't even look at Puffy. I don't think he'd had a bath since our meeting on the beach. He spoke to the ground. "We was hurt that we didn't get invited, Puffy," he said.

Puffy almost whispered. She said, "Fuck off and die." It was the same voice that had greeted Sylvia and me earlier, but it now had hair, claws, and teeth.

Tankhauser saw me and shook his head. "You got your fuckin' nerve, Puffy," he said sorrowfully. "Inviting geeks but not inviting leading members of the beach community such as us."

"Hah," Puffy said. The word was a sharp shaft up the kazoo.

In that subtle endearing way he had, Tankhauser hauled off and hit her with the back of his gloved hand. Everyone in the crowd sucked in his breath. Behind me, somebody began to cry softly. When Puffy took her hands down from her face, they were covered with blood. The silver studs of Tankhauser's glove had opened broad red streaks across her cheek.

My water pistol was in the car. I could not fight Gotterdammerung by myself. I probably couldn't do it even with Puffy's help. It would take a hero to fight six barbarians. I wasn't that much of a hero. I don't think even Philip Marlowe was that much of a hero.

I said, "Let them in, Puffy. A party isn't worth dying for."

"A smart guy," said Wortan, the big guy with all the hair.

"Shut up," Tankhauser said. He pushed past Puffy as if she were a swinging door. Wortan followed, and then the others in their pecking order. The party guests made a path for them, but Gotterdammerung elbowed people out of their way anyhow, just for fun.

Tankhauser turned suddenly and said, "Dollkyrie. Make sure nobody leaves."

Dollkyrie giggled without intelligence and un-wound the chain from where it crossed between her breasts. She swung it casually, and it dragged on the ground as she walked back to the door. Many of the guests were fascinated with the movement of her hips. Dollkyrie was a tall, slim woman wearing jeans, black boots that reached to her knees, and a jerkin of small metal plates. The wings on her helmet looked ridicu-lous, but nobody laughed.

We moved away from her, and I said to Puffy, "You can fumigate after they leave."

She nodded grimly. Blood flowed freely down her face and made growing blots on her dress. She made no move to stop it. I think she liked it. It gave her something to remember them by.

Somebody said, "Call the police."

"Sure," I said. "They'll be here in an hour or two."

Further back in the house we heard a shriek, and then harsh laughter. Something made of glass shat-tered.

"Bastards," Puffy said softly, but with great feeling. She followed after Gotterdammerung.

For a while, they tried on coats. Puffy and I stood in the bedroom doorway watching them. I don't know if I had the illusion I could protect Puffy, or if wild animals fascinated me. Maybe both. Sylvia was sud-denly there between us, watching with the grim ex-pression that had suddenly become fashionable at Puffy's party.

"Do something," Sylvia whispered.

"Maybe I should leap a tall building in a single bound."

"Sure," said Puffy. "That should impress the hell

out of them." She patted my shoulder, leaving a rusty brown smudge on my lime-green coat.

Gotterdammerung-less Dollkyrie paid no more attention to us than a television picture would. Each of them picked up coat after coat, tried it on, then threw it on the floor. They weren't gentle.

Tankhauser and Sickfred ended up wearing bomber jackets that had torn up the back and had sleeves that were tight halfway down their forearms. Wortan was wearing a fur number that was probably a coat owned by some slim local faun. He tied the sleeves around his neck and wore it like a stunted cape. Goonhilda plucked a delicate purple scarf from a pocket and tied it around her head, where sweat caused it to change color. Thor-head never did find anything he liked. In his frustration, he used his big knife to slash wantonly as many coats as he could get his hands on.

Pleased as paper dolls with their new finery, they took all the cups of yoyogurt from the bathtub, and more of them from the refrigerator. They piled the cups around them like medieval towers and demanded music. Music started. While it played, they sprawled across furniture, alternately using their fingers sloppily to eat the yoyogurt and to conduct the music. "Two girls for every boy!" Tankhauser and Wortan growled in voices that belonged in Heavenly Daise's menagerie. Harmony from hell.

My brain tumbled through idea after idea. *If only*, most of them began. *I could just*, a lot of them started. I wore ruts running them by over and over again. I was brave enough to take on all six of them, but not smart enough to come up with a plan that would prevent my getting killed. The plans all required a man who was six feet tall and built like Godzilla. That, or possession of a howitzer. Not one of my plans was of any more use than an upholstered dishpan.

There was a commotion at the front door, and at first I thought the police had arrived. Before I had taken three steps to find out, something came into the short hallway outside the room where the debauch was going on. I was not in the mood to laugh, but what I saw made me laugh.

It was a more or less human-shaped rubber bag full of lumpy fur. A face mask was pushed high onto its sloping forehead. It had not stopped to remove its rubber fins, so it flopped awkwardly down the hall, pistol in one hand, spear gun in the other. There was another way to describe what it was. It was a gorilla in a wet suit.

As difficult as it was to tell one gorilla from another, I was willing to bet my trench coat that I had last seen this very gorilla at the Nurture/Nature Bookstore.

The gorilla lifted the pistol and pointed it at me. My hands went up. The gorilla called out, "Hey, Spike! Look at this!" A minute later two more gorillas shuffled into the hallway, one of them pushing Dollkyrie before him. Her lips moved nervously from side to side beneath angry eyes. She snapped at the nearest gorilla and took a bite from his wet suit, then chewed with satisfaction on the shred of rubber.

Spike said, "We're gonna take care of you good, mister. We were twenty minutes signing autographs in that bookshop. My hand still hurts."

The three gorillas backed me and Dollkyrie into the music room. The music had stopped, and nobody moved to start it again. Gotterdammerung, fermenting in yoyogurt, seemed to lie across the furniture without bones. Trails of yoyogurt led down their chins and beards. I could have taken them now, but it was too late. Now there were the gorillas to deal with.

When Spike saw them, he said, "You guys got no class."

Tankhauser rose a little from the floor and said, "Who ain't got no class?" He really wanted to know.

"You ain't got no class. Get out."

Tankhauser thought about that. It was a long, difficult way from one end of the thought to the other. Then he swore and stood up with all the grace of a drunken camel. He pulled Goonhilda to her feet. They and the others stumbled from the room. A moment later, I heard motorcycle engines. A moment after that, I heard nothing but Puffy's guests taking this opportunity to get together whatever was left of their stuff and make hurried escapes.

I said, "You guys are good. I wish I'd thought of telling those goons to get out."

"It don't work for everybody," Tiger said and laughed. It was the wild, untutored laugh of an idiot. Spike told him to shut up, and he did.

"We're still looking for Heavenly Daise," Spike said.

"It's the national pastime. Bigger than baseball."

"You're a funny guy. You know what else is funny? That every place we look for her, you're right there too."

"Funny," Tiger said.

"We all agree. It's funny."

Sylvia came into the room and said, "There you are, Zoot—" She and the gorillas saw each other at the same moment. The guns wavered, and I jumped for Spike, hoping to knock him against the other two. I knocked Spike's pistol aside as he fired it. Sylvia shrieked and clutched her arm, where a red flower began to bloom. She wilted to the floor. "Sylvia!" I cried. I had Spike by his gun wrist and one shoulder. I had him the way a flea has a dog.

"Sylvia?" Duke said.

"Shut up," Spike said. He stood there for a moment, his gun wavering. He shrugged me off and backed away, his pistol steady again, but pointed in my direction. They all pointed their pistols in my direction until they were gone. I found a pile of cocktail napkins decorated with surfers and made Sylvia hold them against the wound. She held them mechanically, without thought, but she held them.

I ran to the front door and looked outside at the placid water. The diving bell bobbed to the surface, making the water rock between it and the edge of the pool. The gorillas were gone. There was nothing to suggest they'd ever been there but a woman inside the house who had an angry hole in her arm.

When I got back to Sylvia, Puffy was on the floor tipping a glass of water into her. Puffy told me where an emergency room was and threw a heavy blue knitted shawl around Sylvia's bare shoulders. Together, Puffy and I helped her to the diving bell. The captain of the bell looked as if he'd had a long night. Bags under his eyes that had been wallet-size were now steamer trunks. He didn't make any jokes.

The air above ground was cold, and it revived Sylvia enough for her to pull the shawl tighter around herself and to make a pretense of helping us get her into the car. The parking attendants stayed back at their lighted shack, watching us. Puffy was yelling at them as I drove away.

There wasn't much traffic on Pacific Coast Highway that time of night. Driving was the pleasure it always should have been but so rarely was—if my first day of driving in Los Angeles was any indication. I rolled along with an unconscious woman sprawled across my back seat, dripping blood onto Puffy's expensive shawl and from there onto some very ordinary upholstery. The big black animal of the Pacific Ocean played in the dark to my left and told me nothing.

It didn't tell me if the gorillas had shot Sylvia by mistake or because they were after Sylvia as well as Heavenly. It didn't tell me if the mistake the gorillas might have made was in thinking that Sylvia *was* Heavenly or in shooting Sylvia merely because she had surprised them by walking into the room.

It didn't tell me what strange power—yes, that was the correct melodramatic phrase—what strange power the gorillas had over Gotterdammerung. I didn't believe for a moment that Gotterdammerung was impressed by the pistols the gorillas carried. Maybe Gotterdammerung worked for the gorillas. That would tie things together nicely. My problem was that I didn't yet have enough string to make a good strong knot.

CHAPTER 17
No Particular Gorillas

A gangly black youth sat at the end of the waiting room. His arm was in a fresh cast, and he stared at the jolly posters of snow-capped mountains on the wall opposite him without interest or comprehension. It was very late. He'd probably had a busy evening. The room between him and the wall with the poster on it was probably crowded with ghosts.

The emergency room was filled with harsh white light and a chemical smell as harsh as the light, a smell that institutions meant to convey cleanliness but succeeded only in reminding you of other stark, dreary public places. The room was empty but for the black kid and his invisible ghosts, and rows of not very stylish orange chairs whose cushions were cracking on the sides.

I rang a night buzzer, and a young, serious nurse bustled out from between double doors painted the same orange as the chairs. She saw Sylvia, and before I'd had a chance to say anything, she took Sylvia back with her to wherever she'd come from. A few minutes later, another nurse, this one much older, came out and asked me to fill out some forms. She was polite in a way that suggested she didn't have to be polite.

I was sitting there with the pencil and clipboard, wondering what Sylvia's mother's maiden name was, when two hard characters entered. It was a cold night, and they each wore a trench coat but no hat. Nobody in California wears a hat except to ballgames. A uniformed policeman stood in the doorway, casual as a cat at a mousehole.

The taller of the two hard characters had a horse face and enough bushy hair to stuff a pillow. The other one had chubby cheeks and a small, neat mustache. He peered at me through glasses with gold wire frames. They both looked like policemen. The taller one ran his hand through his hair, changing nothing whatsoever, and said, "You Zoot Marlowe?"

"Yes?"

"Puffy Tootsweet was right. That is a bitchen costume." He enjoyed my nose for a moment before he went on, "I'm Sergeant Faraday. This is Officer Davey." Each of them flashed a star at me.

"Glad to meet you. Do either of you know what a maiden name is?"

Sergeant Faraday pulled back as if I'd tried to slap him, then shared a glance with his patrner. He said, "Is this some kind of a rib?"

I had offended him. Philip Marlowe was always offending policemen, and here I was doing the same thing. I said, "Rib? No. But skip it. What can I do for you?"

Officer Davey took that as a cue. He pulled a notebook from a pocket and poised a pen over it. During our conversation, he made notes.

"We answered a call to Puffy Tootsweet's place.

When we got there, she said you were present at the shooting."

"Yes. It was done by a gorilla. One of a matched set of three."

The two men took a long look at me while deciding whether to laugh.

I said, "If you don't believe me, ask Puffy."

"Ms. Tootsweet wasn't in the room when it happened."

"No. But she knows the gorillas were there. If you wait a while, the victim will come out here and tell you about it herself."

Sergeant Faraday raked his hair again and said, "It's OK with us if the shooting was done by an elephant wearing waders." He looked at Officer Davey and growled, "We only get the strange ones, don't we?"

Officer Davey studied me and nodded. He wrote something down, though what it might be I didn't know.

Sergeant Faraday said, "Tell us what happened, Mr. Marlowe." He planted his hands in his pockets.

I told him what had happened from the moment Gotterdammerung arrived. Neither Faraday nor Davey said anything while I spoke. Their faces were as immobile as rocks. Davey took quick notes. When I finished, Faraday said, "Have you seen these gorillas before?"

"Hard to say. All gorillas look alike to me."

"Ever see any gorillas *like* these before?"

"Once at the Surfing Samurai Robots building. Again in a car in West Los Angeles. Again in the Great West Mall."

"What did they want then?"

"Heavenly Daise."

Faraday and Davey read all about that in each other's faces. Faraday said, "Do you know any reason they might want to murder Sylvia Woods?"

"Oh, it's murder now, is it?"

"Attempted murder."

"None. I don't even know why they're looking for Heavenly Daise. Though they seem awfully persistent."

The young nurse came back through the orange double doors guiding Sylvia by one arm. Sylvia's other arm was heavily bandaged and hung in a sling. The blue shawl had been thrown across the whole production and tied in front so it wouldn't fall off. Sylvia's face was slack and white, and she walked as if lead weights were sewn into her party clothes. She tried to smile when she saw me. It was a thin smile, and shook like a cheap violinist's vibrato, but it held. She said, "It looks a lot worse than it is. Just a flesh wound."

I stood with the uniformed policeman while Faraday and Davey sat Sylvia down in a far corner of the room and asked her questions, probably the same questions they'd asked me, if more politely. The black youth turned his head to look at them, but he had problems of his own. He turned his head back and looked across the room at the invisible ghosts again.

The uniformed policeman nodded at me once, slowly, just so that I knew he knew I was there. After that, I looked past him through the square chicken-wire window at the fog rolling in across the parking lot like bad dreams. The red neon emergency sign seemed filled with blood.

Faraday and Davey left Sylvia and came to the door. Faraday thanked me for my cooperation and asked me to come down to the Malibu police station the next

day to make a formal statement. I said I would. The
uniformed policeman already had the door open and
Davey was already outside when Faraday turned back
to me and said, "You have any ideas about where those
gorillas might be now?"

"Not one. But you might ask Samson Andelilah, the
head of security at SSR. He didn't seem to mind that
the gorillas had been snooping around his building."

Faraday ran his hand through the underbrush again
as he said thanks. I watched the three men get into an
unmarked car and drive away. Its headlights momentarily made the fog look as solid as a wall of marble.

Sylvia helped me fill out the forms. Between questions, she stared across the room, which was now as
filled with ghosts for her as it was for the black kid.
We came to the end of it, and the nurse was satisfied,
and I got Sylvia out to the car. She grabbed the knot
of the shawl with her free hand to pull it tighter, then
leaned her good arm against the door.

It was late. The air was heavy with lateness, and
gave each movement, each word, a theatrical flair. Sylvia and I were the only ones still awake and moving
around. Somewhere out there was an audience watching us. Or maybe the day had just been long and com-
plex and I was so tired that nothing seemed real. I
started the engine, turned on the heat, and drove Sylvia home.

Even at this hour, with cars no more frequent than
good ideas, it took almost an hour to drive back to
Hollywood.

For a while, I just drove and Sylvia just sat, winc-
ing now and again when the gentle rocking of the
Chevrolet Belvedere made her arm hurt. I turned up

the long hill at Colorado Boulevard and slowed to a stop at the light at the top.

I said, "How do you feel?"

"With my hands, dummy." I looked across at her. She was smiling wistfully.

"OK," I said, chalking up a point for her. I pushed the car into Santa Monica. We were nearly alone on the street. Bums and street people were standing on the sidewalk in groups, talking or walking around like zombies, or bedding down for the night in doorways through which more respectable people would walk the next morning. As I turned down Lincoln toward the freeway, I said, "Tell me about the gorillas."

"What gorillas?"

"Durf," I said just enough under my breath to make it private.

"Durf?"

"Don't change the subject." She opened her mouth to speak, but I said, "And don't tell me again that all gorillas look alike to you. That doesn't matter. Tell me about any gorillas you've ever had anything to do with. These very particular gorillas seem to know you. Not even gorillas shoot people for nothing."

"You don't have to shout," Sylvia shouted. Her voice was surprisingly strong for a person who'd lost so much blood. Or maybe I was just sensitive.

We drifted past small restaurants and antique shops that had clever names with the word "junque" in them. It was warm in the car, and I cracked a window as I lowered the heat. I turned onto the freeway, and the air began to scream through the open window, but discreetly, as I accelerated down the on-ramp.

Sylvia said, "Heavenly once experimented on a gorilla."

"I'll bet she turned it into a hummingbird."

"She didn't turn it into anything." Sylvia's voice was firm as setting concrete. "She was doing experiments on baldness."

"Did she do anything to the gorilla to make it dislike her?"

Sylvia sighed. I was one dense cookie, I guess. She said, "It was just a regular gorilla, with no more intelligence than gorillas usually have. It didn't wear suits, and it wouldn't know what to do with a gun if it had one."

"Then these three gorillas must be pretty special."

"I suppose," she said without interest.

"Then anybody should be able to recognize these gorillas, even you, who are no good at it."

Sylvia shivered, and I rolled up the window. Heat began to fill the car again. After a while, Sylvia said, "Are you getting at something?"

"Only this: If you'd seen these gorillas before, you'd know it."

"I haven't."

"They obviously know you."

"I look a lot like Heavenly. Didn't you say they were after her?"

I nodded and grumbled yeah. Sylvia was right about everything. She might even be telling the truth. But something about her pat answers made me as nervous as a man about to drive an automobile for the first time.

At the Daise mansion I pulled the car right up to the gate and let Sylvia talk to Davenport, the robotler. The gate swung open, and I drove right up to the front door just as if I were used to driving up to mansions.

Davenport came out while I opened the car door for Sylvia. She clutched the shawl and walked toward the house as if she were made of spun sugar. Davenport was about to follow her when I said, "Davenport?"

"Yes, sir?"

"I'd like to ask Samson Andelilah a few questions."

"Very good, sir."

"I'd like to speak with him tonight, if possible. Can you give me his home phone number?"

"I am not programmed to give out that information."

"You know that I'm working for Mr. Daise?"

"Of course, sir."

"Well?"

"I am not programmed to give out that information."

"Are you programmed to tell Ms. Woods that I will call tomorrow to see how she is?"

"Of course, sir."

"What luck. I found something that you *are* programmed for."

"Yes, sir." Davenport didn't even blink.

Just for my own entertainment, I said, "I'll bet you're a lot of fun at parties."

Davenport didn't say anything. He just watched while I got back into my car and drove away.

Driving back to Malibu took another forty-five minutes and, when I wasn't fighting to keep my eyes open, I had a lot of time to think about missing rich girls and look-alike secretaries and gorillas that made mistakes. I added that together with sabotaged surf-bots and motorcycle maniacs and yoyogurt, and came up with nothing. On the other hand, I was more tired than I remembered being in a long time. On the other hand, maybe I wasn't programmed for detective work. On the other hand, if I kept this up, I'd run out of hands.

I waved hands at myself until I got back to the house. Some hands were more popular than others. None of them was helpful. Across from the house the stoplight blinked to itself. It reflected off the windows of Sylvia's boxy blue car, which was still parked out in front, now looking cold and lonely. Even before I opened the front door, I heard music and laughter. When I opened the door, it assaulted me. The music and noise were not nearly as loud as the party at Puffy Tootsweet's, but it was late and I was easier to assault than I had been earlier.

I found all of them in the living room. They'd piled the pillows into one corner and thrown the other junk up against the walls in drifts. In the center of the floor, a cross stick hung about three feet off the floor on two not very sturdy uprights. Just outside each upright was a bowl with some flame in it.

Hanger was jerking her shoulders in time with the music as she approached the setup and tried to bend backward far enough to dance under it. Her tits knocked the cross stick onto the floor, and everybody whooped. Captain Hook seemed to be having as good a time as anybody else. Clever boy. If he put his mind to it, he didn't need Puffy Tootsweet.

Nobody saw me standing in the shadow at the end of the hallway. That pleased me. I backed away from the noise and the light and went into Whipper Will's bedroom, where I lay down on a pile of clothes and wondered how long the party would keep me awake. I didn't even finish the thought before I slid like a greased seal into quiet and darkness.

CHAPTER 18
Back to the Salt Mines

I awoke to someone banging on the front door—from the outside, I thought. I stumbled to my feet, took note that Whipper Will and Bingo had tangled themselves together with the sheets as they slept, and went to see what all the ruckus was about.

It was about six-and-a-half feet tall and wearing a gold coverall with the name Lenny squiggled in blue on the breast pocket. A stub of dead cigar stuck out of its face. "SSR," Lenny mumbled as if he were not very happy about having to say it. He was delivering a crate that was big enough to house a small dog. He hefted it in both hands, though he could have carried it under one arm, and took it into the living room, where he set it down next to the sticks.

He looked around at the mess and at the sleeping surfers and sniffed. "What is this place?" he said.

"The Malibu the tourists never see," I said.

He only sneered at me. After all, I was a customer. "There's your box," he said and handed me something on a clipboard to sign. When I was done, he took his clipboard and stomped back along the hall with it.

I closed the door on his truck starting and went back to the living room.

Using some tools I eventually found in the kitchen, I got the crate open. Inside were a few miles of bubble wrap. Inside that was Bill, the SSR robot duck. Even in that living room, not the brightest place in the world, Bill shone like the Moon on water.

A sticker big enough to play polo on was plastered to the top of Bill's shiny silver head. It told me that to activate Bill I should pull off the sticker. No other instructions were necessary. Bill was entirely self-contained, and would explain himself. That sounded like famous last words. I pulled off the sticker.

Bill turned his head to look at me. He blinked, which was a nice touch, and said, "Hiya, Marlowe. Where are the girls?"

"What girls?"

"Any girls. I'm not fussy."

"I don't remember ordering a robot with a sex drive."

"Standard equipment."

"Sure. Wait here. I'll be right back."

I called SSR and asked to talk to Lance in sales. Lance came on the line, sounding as breathy and energetic as if I'd caught him in the shower. I told him that I didn't want a robot with an interest in girls. Or with an interest in anything but doing what it was told. Lance thought that Bill might need adjustment. I could bring him in any time next week.

"Bring him in? Next week? Is that what you call service?" I said.

"Service with a smile," he said, showing all his teeth, even through the phone.

"I call it the big rah-zoo." I hung up, thought for a

moment, then called SSR again. This time I asked for Samson Andelilah. A few minutes later a voice like a French horn said, "Security. Andelilah speaking." I imagined the enormous man sitting behind the desk in a room full of smoke. He'd frown as he put down his cigarette for a moment to answer the phone.

"Mr. Andelilah? This is Zoot Marlowe, the industrial spy from Bay City."

"Yes, Mr. Marlowe?" The beautiful voice was flat and polite, not wanting or expecting anything.

"You remember me?"

"Of course."

"And the three I was brought in with, in fur coats?"

"Yes."

"Did I call at a bad time, Mr. Andelilah? Are you, maybe, lighting a cigarette?" I could hear him breathing slowly, thoughtfully.

"Cut to the chase, Marlowe," Andelilah said.

"What do you know about those gorillas?"

"Nothing at all."

"Did you know, for instance, that last night one of them took a shot at Sylvia Woods, the Daises' social secretary?"

He breathed at me some more and said, "It wouldn't matter if they'd burned down the SSR factory. I don't know anything about them." He hung up. Not an angry hang, but a gentle click. It all came to the same thing: more work for Zoot Marlowe.

I went back into the bedroom. Whipper Will and Bingo had changed positions. If they'd been standing up, they would have been doing a pretty impressive ballet step. Horizontal, it wasn't much. I changed out of my party clothes and put on my brown suit. I didn't feel so much like a goof now.

When I got back to the living room, Bill was whispering into Flopsie's (or was it Mopsie's?) ear. Whatever he was saying fascinated her. I said, "The entire SSR corporation is busy at the moment. Probably polishing the demonstrators in the showroom. You'll have to learn to control yourself."

"Anything you say."

"You're probably programmed to say that."

"Anything you say." Bill let out a mechanical cackle from deep in his spherical body. He stopped abruptly and blinked at me.

"All right. Come on."

"Where are you going?" Mopsie (or was it Flopsie?) said.

"Back to the salt mines."

The girl looked confused, and I said, "Tell Captain Hook he's getting his money's worth."

She smiled and nodded, pleased to be trusted with such an important message.

Bill waddled after me and hopped into the passenger side of the Belvedere. He looked around as if everything interested him. From behind the wheel I said, "How are you at geography?"

"Local or international?"

"Local. Fairly local. Say, the streets between here and San Diego."

"All in the ol' bubble memory," Bill said as he tapped the side of his head with a very finger-like wing tip.

"Tell me how to get to the Malibu police station."

He reeled off street names so fast I couldn't follow them. After I got him to slow down, we both did better. In ten minutes, I was pulling into the parking lot of a one-story brick building with a glass door and big picture windows. Inside, I asked for Sergeant Faraday. Faraday came to the desk and led me back to his office, a cavernous industrial-green room he shared with about three other guys, none of whom was there at the moment, just their desks. The room was clean, but shabby with use, and with furniture supplied by the lowest bidder. The place smelled like dust. Old dust.

He got me settled in a wooden chair that had cigarette burns on the edges of the arms and called in a stenographer. She wore a tent-like brown dress and practical shoes. The spot of rouge on each soft cheek gave her wrinkled old face all the life of a wax dummy. She had been a stenographer for a long time, maybe starting with chisels and clay tablets. Not even Bill would be interested in making lewd suggestions to her.

While she took notes, I talked for twenty minutes by the caged clock on the wall, answering Sergeant Faraday's questions about the shooting as best I could. When we were done, I said, "I hope you won't make Sylvia Woods drive all the way out here in her condition."

Faraday looked pained. "You private guys think you're the only ones who are human." He peered at me as if he were trying to guess my weight. "You always wear that costume?"

"It's kind of a religious thing."

"I got a friend at Cal Tech who I think would like to take you apart."

"Not unless he has a warrant. What about Sylvia Woods?"

"We'll talk to her on the phone."

"Good. You're not a bad guy, Faraday."

"You're not a bad guy either, Marlowe. But some of that patter is a little stale."

"Not stale," I said. "Just aged in the keg."

He nodded, appreciating the wit of my remark, but mostly waiting for me to stand up and leave. But I wasn't ready to do that yet. I said, "What about the gorillas?"

"No word yet."

"No leads? No rumors? No traces? No nothing?"

"We'll find them," Faraday said with the kind of determination that won the West.

"If you look for them."

"What does that mean?"

"That means that unless there's some cranny along this coast that you don't know about, those gorillas have more protection than gorillas ought to have."

The shutters went down behind Faraday's eyes. His face was as blank as a plaster doll's. He said, "But you're just supposing."

I nodded. "Kind of an intellectual exercise."

Coolly, Faraday said, "When we find those gorillas, I'm going to jam them down your throat."

I waved my hand in front of my nose and said, "There's a lot of stale patter in here today."

He chewed on me with his eyes for a moment and then told me to get out. I went. Bill was hanging out the window watching girls scamper across the sand to the ocean with their towels and radios.

I asked him to guide me to Huntington Beach and gave him the address of *Brown Genes Magazine*. The lights in his eyes went out for a moment. When they snapped back on, he said, "My meat, Marlowe," and he told me to head south.

* * *

One little beach town blended seamlessly into the next. The weather was fine, with a high blue sky over one picture postcard scene after another showing prime beachfront property. Huntington Beach had its share of walk-up food emporiums, T-shirt shops, and sporting goods stores. Surf-bots were being featured by nobody.

Bill told me to slow down, and a moment later I saw the place, a small white stucco building in the hip pocket of a pod mall. Plastic letters looking not much like driftwood and spelling BROWN GENES MAGA-ZINE hung over a storefront that might have been a taco joint before, and might be again.

A small car such a pale shade of pink that I could have imagined the pink almost backed into me. I got glared at by some very big and shiny sunglasses, and then the car shot out into traffic looking for a good place to have an accident.

I parked in the empty spot and asked Bill to come with me. I dragged Bill past an ice cream fountain and a photocopy store. I had to drag him because he wanted to stop and see what was happening in each place. There were no women in the photocopy store, so maybe he was just curious. When we got to the magazine office, the door was open. I went in with Bill at my heels.

The office smelled like a lot of old paper floating on a faint sweet cloud that leaked in from the ice cream shoppe next door. It was a long room with a white rectangle at the back that would be an open door. Fluorescent lights, which ran from side to side, bled personality from everything in the room.

Three large metal desks, one behind the other, were lined up on each side of the room, all facing front. Each desk had a tower of organizing baskets, some of them overflowing onto a desk that was already crowded with paper and pencils. Back in one corner was a private office made by partitions that did not go all the way to the acoustical-tiled ceiling. The door was closed.

Between the front desks and the office, a long row of sheets with writing and sketches was taped to the wall. Above the long row of sheets were posters of surf-bots surfing. More posters just like them faced them from the wall opposite.

At one of the back desks, a blond kid was typing madly, studying the ceiling, then typing madly again. He wore a very crisp blue short-sleeved shirt that was pretty conservative for his crowd. The only pattern on it was black silhouettes of palm trees.

At the front desk was a girl with the same color hair as the kid who was typing, but long enough so that it did not stop at her shoulders. She wore a T-shirt that said SURF TILL YOU'RE RAW! under a picture of a surfer with lots of teeth and some very buggy eyes. She was using a blue pencil to cross things out angrily on a sheet of not very neat typing.

Without looking up, she cried, "Can you crank it a little, Frankie?"

The kid in the back, who must have been Frankie, cried, "Aarrggh!" as he tossed his hands into the air, caught them, and typed madly again.

I said, "Excuse me."

The girl jumped as if I'd goosed her and glared at me. She was cute and had the half-wise look of someone young enough not to realize she had a lot to learn. She ran a finger back to hook her blond hair over one

ear and remembered her manners. "Can I help you?"
she said.

"You bet," Bill said and took a step forward. I
grabbed him around the throat. Not too hard. Bill
didn't even struggle.

"Ever hear of a robot with a hormone problem?" I
said and smiled. When she did not smile back I said,
"I'm interested in some information about one of your
subscribers."

"Are you the police?" The thought that I might be
a policeman worried her. I wondered, in an offhanded
way, what she had to hide.

"No. I'm a private detective working on a case."

"Just like on the late-late show."

"Yeah. I've been hired by my client to find his
daughter. She subscribes to your magazine. I thought
she might have sent you a change of address so that
she could still get it."

She said, "I'm sorry. We don't give out that kind
of information to just anybody." Already her blue
pencil was poised over her copy. When I didn't say
anything she ran a tongue over her lower lip and did
not look happy. She said, "We have access to the database, of course, over the phone lines from Sub-Tech
in Glendale. But they won't give it to you either. Our
subscription list is a valuable commodity."

"Gack," Bill said, trying to speak. I squeezed a little
tighter, then loosened up immediately. I was adjust-
ing Bill in my own way, but I didn't want to hurt him.

"Valuable," I said. "You mean I could buy it?"

"For about a thousand dollars. Maybe. Slink would
have to decide."

"Slink Silverman, the editor," I said, quoting from
the issue of *Brown Genes* I'd seen.

"That's right."

"Suppose somebody not very nice offered you a lot of money for that list?"

She scowled, barely creasing her face, and said, "We're very careful about who we sell the list to." The blue pencil was tapping the paper now in a counterpoint to the typing coming from the back of the room. If I'd been in the mood, I would have danced.

"Thanks for the information," I said. "I'll talk to my client." She nodded at me and bent her head over the copy again. I said, "Just one more thing."

She looked up, surprised I hadn't vanished instantly in a puff of smoke. "Yes?"

"What about surf-bots?"

The fearful look I'd seen when I'd mentioned the police came back. She sat very stiffly now, the buttons of her tits tight against the material of her T-shirt. The typing had stopped, and Frankie was looking in our direction. "Surf-bots?" she said.

"Sure," I said. "Like in the pictures on your walls."

"Mister," she said as if she were repeating a formula she had carefully memorized, "there isn't anybody around here who knows anything about surf-bots."

"What about you, Frankie?"

"Nada," he said but did not continue his typing.

For a moment, we were a room full of people pretending that surf-bots had never existed. I said, "I guess the disappearance of surf-bots all over town is too much like news for this rag." They were still watching as I carried Bill out the door.

I let Bill down on the sidewalk, and he moved his head as if his neck were stiff. He said, "What a babe!"

and I grunted. He smacked his lips a few times as we walked slowly back to my car and got in.

The car was a box full of heat, and we rolled down the windows to let some of it out. Just to hear myself talk, I said, "I could ask Mr. Daise for a thousand bucks to buy the subscription list, but that doesn't seem very elegant."

"No problem," Bill said.

I looked across the seat at him. His feet didn't dangle over the floor only because they didn't reach the edge of the seat. He was looking at me, his eyes bright. Or that could have been reflected sunlight. He said, "You don't need a thousand bucks. You just need me. Your friendly native guide."

CHAPTER 19
What Goes Around Comes Around

Bill gave me directions, but he wouldn't tell me where we were going. "Trust me," he kept on saying.

I said, "I understand that in Hollywood, 'trust me' means 'fuck you.' "

"Trust me," he said again and laughed his gravel-guts laugh.

A few blocks from the magazine office he told me to park in front of a big square cement building, which may once have been some color other than the color of ancient cement. It was surrounded by a chain-link fence protecting nothing but the building and some industrious crabgrass that had not been troubled lately. The fence had never done much of a job, judging by the gang graffiti sprayed all over the front of the building. Chiseled high over the door was the motto "What Goes Around Comes Around." I could tell it was fancy work because the U's were pointed at the bottom.

"Well?" I said.

"Maybe you've heard that Los Angeles used to have a rapid transit system."

"I understand certain interests would rather sell cars."

"That's what they say. They also say that these same interests know how to make cars that run on farts and tires tougher than a mailman's corns."

"Can I just get the good-parts version of the story?" I said.

"OK," Bill said. "Without the local color, it comes down to this. A few years ago some civic-minded types decided Los Angeles needed a subway system. They built some stations and some track, none of which actually went anywhere. The civic-minded types made their money and went home."

"This is one of the stations. So?"

"So. Empty track isn't the only thing we have down there. Come on." He got out of the car and walked toward the fence. Being the curious type, I got out of the car and followed him. He cast up and back along the fence like a dog looking for a scent. A moment later, he crawled under the fence where some juvenile delinquent had bellied it up and walked toward the building.

Traffic drifted by in another universe, apparently not paying any attention to us or to what we did. Best not to notice. Somebody else's business. Don't get involved. A moment later, I was walking across the crabgrass after Bill.

Then Bill was gone. I wanted to call out his name, but some reserve of caution stopped me. It did not stop me from walking through the same weed patch where Bill had gone. But slowly. Snails passed me. At last I came to a pair of double doors. They were thick and made of some heavy metal that was decomposing in green flakes. Some artist had taken a great deal of time with those doors, sculpting into them a fancy filigree of trains, boats, planes, cars. Maybe the spiders appreciated it.

Bill stuck his head out from around one of the doors, which had looked closed but was open a little. He said, "You coming, or what?" and disappeared. I went around the corner of the door after him.

Bill and I were standing in a dim dank place lit only by the weak efforts of the sun—too wise to try harder—that came in through high brown-tinted windows in long dust-filled shafts. The walls were covered with tile that at one time may have been a sunny yellow. The tile may have once covered the walls and not had great patches missing, showing heavy wire mesh behind it. It may once have not been dripping with long brown stains that looked like continents better left undiscovered. Somewhere, water was still dripping—drop by slow, tedious drop.

Electric sconces in the shape of animals lined the walls like gargoyles. The floor was covered with old hamburger wrappers and soft drink cups and beer cans and glass bottles of various sizes and shapes, from the improbably expensive to the conspicuously tawdry, and the remains of campfires and camps and of human metabolism.

Overlaying the smell of civilization's castoffs was the smell of dirty water that had stood too long—a thick damp mucky smell that would grow mushrooms under your arms if you stayed in it long enough.

"I guess it was either this or Disneyland, eh Bill?"

"Do you want that subscription list, or don't you?" He walked across the tile floor, making marks in the thin gruel of dust and rancid water that covered it. I picked my way after him, avoiding the worst of the refuse.

Soon, we were beyond the area where the weak brown light could reach, and Bill's eyes glowed like headlights. I looked where he looked because that's where the light was. We walked down wide stairs to one of the boarding levels. There were still ads for cigarettes and coffee on the walls, prettied up with mustaches and sex organs and the same old suggestions.

I pulled my trench coat tighter around myself against the cold. It was not the civilized cold of the SSR lobby, but a cold of despair and slug-like unclean things you might find under a rock in a graveyard. A cold to make you wake up screaming if you remembered it in your dreams some bad night.

"Down here," Bill said, and he jumped off the platform onto a narrow walkway next to the track. We walked along, Bill's headlights picking out the rails as they curved into the distance. Between the rails was a thin snake of water. Every sound we made was magnified until it sounded as if we were walking through hell with an army of goblins.

I whispered, "Are you sure you know where you're going?"

"Bubble memory," Bill whispered back.

"Sure. Standard equipment."

"How else?"

"But why? SSR can't think the average customer would be crawling around under the city."

"You'd be amazed how much room there is in here," he tapped the side of his head. "I know things you'd never think of asking me. But somebody else might. We go down here." Bill climbed down a metal ladder. The crossbars sang with each step he took.

We climbed down a long shaft and came out in a

square corridor hung with pipes, conduits, and cables. It was much like the corridor under the SSR building, but dirtier. I could feel the weight of the city over my head. I followed Bill and stopped suddenly.

"What's that?" I said.

Not far enough away I could hear scratching noises.

"They won't bother us. They don't like the light. Just a little farther."

I wondered who "they" were while I counted a hundred steps to where Bill stopped before a metal cabinet like hundreds of others we'd passed. Thick cables ran into and out of it. Stenciled on it were the words Beach Cities Telephone and a serial number. While I read the words, I heard more scratching sounds, closer now. I said, "Do what you have to do."

"Right." Bill had me open the metal cabinet. It wasn't locked. Why should it be? Inside was a computer keyboard and a small screen. A small iris opened in Bill's round body, and a cable snaked out. Its end fit pretty well into a female plug next to the screen.

Bill tapped on the keyboard, and columns of letters and numbers rolled across the screen. Bill studied them, tapped some more. Soon, the screen cleared but for the word Working. A few seconds later came the words Database Copied. Bill tapped some more, and the screen went blank as a blind eye. The cable reeled back into his body.

"Got it?" I said.

"Got it." He turned, ready to lead us back to the surface, when his headlights fell on the dry, scaly body of a fat white alligator that was blocking the corridor the way we'd come. It opened its mouth and hissed at us. I would have hissed back, but I had forgotten how.

CHAPTER 20
Hello, Marlowe, Hello

"I thought it didn't like the light," I said.

"Take another look," Bill said. "It doesn't have any eyes."

"What's back that way?" I pointed in the direction we had been going. The alligator must have sensed the movement because it hissed again and moved its head. Or the moving and hissing could have been coincidental. I had my hopes.

"More corridor," Bill said.

"That's good enough for me."

We shuffled backward. The alligator clambered forward after us. It didn't move very fast, but it kept up.

"What does this guy normally eat?" I said.

"You'd be amazed what people flush down their toilets."

"You'd be amazed what wouldn't amaze me. Can we move a little faster? That dragon's breath is taking the crease out of my pants."

"Not unless you carry me."

I carried him.

All I could hear now was the sound of my own running footsteps and of my own breathing. All I could see was in the cone of light thrown by Bill's eyes. All I thought about was that beast behind us. They were enough. I was a busy guy.

After I'd run around the equator a few times, we came to a metal ladder like the one we'd climbed down before. I looked back and saw the alligator a few yards away and closing. Something behind us hissed. I turned quickly and saw another albino alligator coming from the direction we'd been going. Without asking permission, I tucked Bill under one arm and climbed the metal ladder. It sang about foundries and fear and other F words.

I stood at the top of the shaft breathing hard. Air moving in and out of my lungs could not cover the wild thrashing sound coming from below as the alligators fought. There was an occasional clang as one of them knocked against the ladder. Suddenly the fight was over. Something below hissed. Whether in pain or in triumph, I could not tell. Maybe the two alligators just decided to shake hands and go about their business. Maybe, but I doubted it.

"You can put me down now," Bill said. I put him down.

Bill led us back to the surface. We came out in a different subway station. This one had pale blue tile, and the garbage was in different places, but it was different only in details. This station was run down, full of plenty of nothing and smelled bad, just like the other one. The front door was locked, but not very, and we pushed our way out, breaking the old lock as we did it. I almost kissed the crabgrass when we got out into the bright sunlight.

On the long walk back to the car, Bill said, "You

took a big chance climbing that ladder without asking me. It could have led anywhere."

"*Up* was all I wanted." I shook my head and said, "Why would anybody pay *Brown Genes* big bucks for their subscription list?"

"Let me guess," said Bill. "Because *Brown Genes* asks for it?"

"Sure. But how many people can want their list?"

"Not many. That sweetie at the magazine could have saved us a lot of trouble if she'd thought of that."

I smiled, imagining I looked bold and romantic. "Trouble," I said, "is my business."

The drive up the coast to Malibu was long and hot. Traffic seemed to explode from the street, more of it all the time. Before we got back to the house, I had taken off my trench coat and hat and loosened my tie. Even Bill looked frazzled.

Sylvia's car was gone. Somebody must have come to drive it home.

The big news was that there was no news. Whipper Will and the rest were lying on towels in the small red brick backyard between the house and the public walkway. They had towels over their eyes against the bright sky. Beyond the public walkway lay the sand, a great unmade bed. Here and there, a group sat clustered on a blanket, looking out to sea.

I leaned out the back door and said, "What's the haps, paps?"

Without moving anything but his mouth, Captain Hook said, "Workin' on my tan, man. What about you?"

"More clues," I said. "Not many answers."

"Surf-O-Rama's in a couple days, dude."

"Yeah." I went back into the house and used the

phone in the kitchen to call the Daise mansion. Davenport answered the phone.

"How's Ms. Woods?" I said.

"Mending nicely, sir."

"That's good. Can I speak to her?"

"Not possible, sir. She's gone out."

"Out? In her condition?"

"She is not a prisoner here, sir."

"No." I thought for a moment. I must have thought longer than Davenport was programmed to wait because he said, "Is there anything else, sir?"

"Ms. Woods's car is no longer here."

"One of the security guards and I picked it up this morning, sir."

"Good enough." We each said good-bye and hung up. I stood there with my hand on the receiver long enough for Bill to ask me if there was something wrong.

"Yeah. This whole thing stinks. And for a guy with a nose like mine, that can be a problem."

"What else is new?"

"Let's find out." I took Bill back to Whipper Will's bedroom where we stepped around the pile of clothes until we came to where the computer sat on a table.

"Does that look familiar to your bubble memory?" I said.

"Sure. It's a Rotwang 5000. A sweet little machine."

"Let's see if that subscription list is worth the money we didn't pay for it."

Bill nodded and hopped onto the chair in front of the machine. The cable snaked out of his body as it had before. Bill had me reach around behind the machine and plug the cable in. I switched on the Rotwang 5000. Bill stiffened for a moment and then relaxed.

As he had in the tunnels below Huntington Beach, Bill played with the keys on the keyboard. He answered questions, made numbers come and go on the screen. It all meant as much to me as the pattern of sun sparkles on a choppy sea. I sat on the edge of the bed to wait, wishing I had a pipe or a cigarette so that I could peer through the smoke as it rose in curls to the ceiling. The smell in Samson Andelilah's office came back to me, and I rubbed my nose. What did Philip Marlowe see in smoking?

The computer made a noise like a bird, and names and addresses rolled across the screen much too quickly to be read, even if somebody were good at it.

Bill spoke to me over his shoulder. "What exactly are we looking for? I say exactly because this machine doesn't deal too well with maybes."

"Can you make it look for a particular word?"

"Sure."

"Make it look for Daise." I spelled the name for him.

Bill did some more fancy typing. The machine made small noises to itself, as if someone were shuffling paper clips inside it. A moment later, a screenful of subscribers came up with the small lighted bar flashing under the first letter of the line in the middle of the page. The line said: DAISE, HEAVENLY 14263 LOMA ALTA VISTA DEL ORO MALIBU CA

I took a sheet of paper and a pencil from my pocket and wrote down the address.

"That's it. Thanks."

"You want to save this list for something? Maybe we could sell it." More nuts and bolts died as he laughed.

"You sell it. I'm going visiting." I stood up, threw my imaginary cigarette to the floor, and stepped on it.

Bill typed and the screen went blank. "Gone forever," he said. "If you want another copy, you go down into that terrible place alone."

"I never liked to be alone."

"Me neither." Bill stood up and stretched his little metal body as if he'd done a day's work, though what a little metal body would have to stretch, I don't know. "Let's go visiting," he said.

We were heading for the garage when the telephone rang. I stood at the front door with my hand on the knob. I could have turned it and walked out, but I didn't. I waited. The phone kept ringing. I was just about to go answer it myself when somebody came in from outside and picked it up. A moment later Bingo called out, "Zoot!"

"Yeah?" I called.

"It's for you."

I walked down the hall thinking about who might be calling me. Not many people had my number. In the kitchen I looked at the phone waiting on the counter. Just waiting there for me, and for no reason at all it had taken on the appearance of an ominous creature. I stood there for a moment, waiting for my hand to decide to pick up the receiver. When it did, I had to swallow once before I said, "Hello?"

"Hello, Marlowe?"

"Yes?"

"I never thought I'd get the chance to say 'Hello, Marlowe' to anybody." The voice was old and comfortable and had a swing all its own.

"Just to people named Marlowe. Hello, Mr. Chesnik."

"How did you know it was me?"

"A lucky guess. What can I do for you?"

"Always with the patter." The volume of his voice went into a dive, and I caught only the first few words of what he said next. "What I called about is humna humna humna. . . ."

I asked Mr. Chesnik to speak up.

"You can't be too careful," he said. Then he went on, his voice a harsh whisper, "You asked me to call you if I heard anything about surf-bots."

"Good memory." He liked the patter. I'd patter at him.

"Good enough. Yes, good enough." He wet his lips with a smack, and said, "Big things are going on at a warehouse downtown."

"How big?"

"Big enough for a *pisher* like you." On Chesnik's end of the phone, the compressor began to chug. Over it, Chesnik said, "SSR has hired a lot of people to help them with a project. They weren't too specific, but I think it has something to do with surf-bots."

"What makes you think that?"

"I been in this business a long time. I got an instinct."

"They hire you too?"

"Another lucky guess."

"What's the address of the warehouse?"

"You don't need it. You can come with me. Anybody asks, you're just hired help."

"Reading those Chandler books has done you some good," I said.

"A good memory. Come soon. We don't want to be late for our shift."

I thanked him and hung up.

Bill said, "What's the good word?"

"Clue. That's a good word," I said over my shoulder. I was halfway down the hall. In a second I was in Whipper Will's room looking for work clothes. I found a blue cotton shirt and a pair of cutoff jeans. The shirt ballooned around me, but the jeans, cut off as they were, were about the right length. My shoes would have to do.

Bill had watched me change. He said, "You figure visiting that address will be heavy work?"

"We're not visiting that address. At least, not right now." I walked fast to where the car was.

"I thought you wanted to find Heavenly Daise."

"I found her. If she has a mailing address, she probably isn't in much trouble. On the other hand, it looks as if my surf-bots are about to boil over."

It was about midafternoon by the time I pulled up in front of Acme Robots. The place did not look any more prosperous than it had the first time. When we got out of the car, Benny began to bark through the fence. Then he forgot about it and sat down to scratch behind one ear.

Mr. Chesnik opened the front door and hurried us inside. He seemed to be dressed in the same sweater and slacks as he had been the last time I'd seen him. His hair was still perfect. In the dim light, he squinted through his glasses at Bill and said, "Who's this?"

"The robot duck you paid for. His name's Bill."

"Can we trust him?"

"He's an SSR robot. You tell me."

Mr. Chesnik shook his head as he laughed a little to himself. It was not an energetic laugh, but it did the job. He stopped abruptly and said, "Come on. We don't want to be late."

CHAPTER 21
Hired Help

Mr. Chesnik led us through the stuffy garage to the fenced-in yard. Benny bounded over to us, got a whiff of me, and backed away. Mr. Chesnik said, "Bad Benny! Bad dog." We piled into the old Oldsmobile and soon were out on the street with Benny, locked up behind the gate barking and scratching.

Nobody said anything as Mr. Chesnik drove up Venice Boulevard to the freeway and then east. Traffic was heavy going our way, but it was as nothing compared to the stuff going west. Going west the traffic looked like mile after mile of parking lot. All that high-priced flash, all dressed up and nowhere to go.

We got off at Alameda and turned north into the industrial district. Heat and dust rose from asphalt that had been corrugated by the weight of heavy trucks that climbed over the street day and night. Mr. Chesnik swore as the Oldsmobile jumped in and out of potholes and over long bumpy stretches. To make the ride even more interesting, railroad tracks ran down the middle of the street, shiny as the stripe on a headwaiter's pants. Big tractor-trailer trucks roared around us like lions fighting over meat.

"I hate downtown," Mr. Chesnik said as he wrestled with his steering wheel.

"There must be worse places," I said.

"Find one," he said and pulled up to a red light. A truck pulled up beside us like a building, rolling on wheels that came halfway up our windows. The truck's engine gargled gravel until the light turned green, then began to move forward so slowly, it barely seemed to be moving at all.

Knots of men stood in doorways. They wore shabby clothes with dirtier places at the wrists and elbows. Some men were talking or even shouting at each other. Mostly they stood, waiting for something that would never happen, and they knew it would never happen. The smell of cooking grease came over the heat like cheap devils looking for Hell.

Further up there was nobody on the sidewalks but the occasional man or woman dressed for business and walking past warehouses very quickly. Mr. Chesnik turned a corner onto a street where warehouses lined up on either side, getting smaller until they met in the distance. Mr. Chesnik said, "Union Station is around here somewhere. You remember?"

"Yeah. It's in *Playback*."

"A terrible book. Chandler should have stopped before he wrote it."

"Sometimes it's hard to stop."

Mr. Chesnik glanced at me and said nothing, but grunted fairly eloquently.

We came to a warehouse where a lot of men were rushing around, carrying clipboards, pushing dollies, all busy and intent on their business. Mr. Chesnik pulled up to a barrier next to a guard station in the shape of an upended shoe box and spoke to the guard who stepped out the door. He was an SSR guard, and he looked a lot more awake than the guy in the SSR lobby. The guard peered into the car and said, "They work for you?"

"Hired help," Mr. Chesnik said. He shrugged.

The guard shook his head, but he stepped back into the guard station to push a button that raised the barrier. We drove into what looked like a small town of warehouses. Racing among them was a pack of small, powerful vehicles—Mr. Chesnik called them forklifts—their engines whining about all the heavy lifting they were doing.

A guard waved us to the right. Further on, another guard waved us into a parking lot where a lot of cars and trucks were already standing. We followed a crowd of men through a gate at one end of the parking lot. I wish I had a nickel for every glance Bill and I got.

With the other men, we walked into a warehouse where there were six or eight lines to get into. We chose one and stood in it.

"This is my hired help," Mr. Chesnik said when he got to the front of the line.

The man on the other side of the table wore crisp work clothes that had never seen work heavier than pushing a pencil, but he had a face that had once been used as a dance floor. Sparse reddish hair was slicked down in waves across his lumpy head. He took a look at me and Bill and mumbled something about the trouble being an equal opportunity employer. But he gave each of us a yellow slip and told us to move along.

Mr. Chesnik read his yellow slip and said, "I got the office."

I had warehouse A-2. Bill had the same. Bill and I

each shook hands with Mr. Chesnik and thanked him. He said, "I wish you luck."

"You think we'll need it?"

"You'll need that and more, *schweetheart.*" He laughed as if that were funny and was still laughing to himself when he turned and walked toward the office. Bill and I went to look for warehouse A-2.

Warehouse A-2 was nothing special, just a big metal box where people with big secrets could keep them. We checked in with the foreman, a tall thin man with a long face and plenty of jaw. He wore a dirty white coat over his clothes and carried a clipboard, but I never saw him look at it. He said his name was Barbles and that we'd get along just fine if we did our work. He sneered at Bill and said, "You ain't no heavy-duty 'bot."

"I'm small but I'm wiry," Bill said. "Wiry, get it?" Bill tried out his laugh on Barbles but got nowhere. Barbles just looked at him.

Then he looked at me. "You ain't so heavy-duty yourself."

I just smiled at him. When the smile penetrated into his brain, Barbles swore and told us to each take a dolly and transport crates from the warehouse onto one of the waiting trucks.

I looked over at the truck being loaded. It was unmarked but for a serial number on the cab door. SSR was keeping a low profile.

We joined the conga line of men pushing empty dollies back into the big cool space of the warehouse. We each had a turn taking a crate loaded by a couple of beefy guys who should have been big enough to satisfy even Barbles.

The crates were the size and shape of coffins. And after pushing one of them on a dolly at too low an angle, I found out that they were heavy. I accidentally pushed my dolly into a pallet of cardboard boxes, and the guy behind me growled at me to watch it.

I walked my crate across the metal tail the truck had let down and into the truck, where the dolly rumbled angrily on the distressed wooden floor. Two beefy guys who might have been the brothers of the guys at the other end manhandled the crate off the dolly, and another guy stacked it neatly. While I took a breath and waited for my arms to stop shaking, one of the manhandlers told me to move along.

"How you doing?" I asked Bill as I rolled the empty cart back into the warehouse.

"Hey, look, if you think hiking around in that sewer again would help, let me know."

"Yeah." I took a sudden right turn between crates stacked over my head, and kept pushing my dolly down the narrow passage. Somebody who I hoped was Bill was right behind me. I didn't have time to look. Not yet.

The first chance I got, I turned left along another narrow passage, moving back into the warehouse. The sounds of men working grew dim with distance, and with the walls of crates between them and me. I turned right the first chance I got, and then left again, always with somebody behind me. At last I came to the wall of the warehouse. It was made of corrugated iron covered with dents and skid marks and scratches that told me it had been treated as gently as an old pipe wrench. I turned and looked at Bill. Bill was looking at me, waiting.

I said, "I need to get inside one of these crates. Any ideas?"

"Just one," he said. He stood up his dolly and went to one of the crates nearest us, rubbing his hands together. He then stuck the edge of his beak into the crack between the crate and its lid. He worked his beak up and back like a crowbar and soon, after not making more noise than the *Inner Sanctum* squeaking door, he pried the lid loose.

"That's a hell of an idea," I said. I put my hands on the lid and held them there, not moving. I listened for the sounds of somebody coming to investigate the noise. I heard men working, but that was all. The squeaking had been one more industrial noise in a world full of industrial noises.

I lifted the lid off and saw just about what I had expected to see. Inside the crate was a golden surf-bot packed in plastic foam cut to fit him exactly. He wore an SSR band around his head and a very small yellow bathing suit that made the gold of his body look dingy. Next to him, on edge in another foam compartment, was a white surfboard. The robot's blue eyes were open and looking at me, or through me to nothing at all.

Stapled to the outside of the box was a flat plastic bag with papers inside. I looked through the plastic at the top sheet and saw that this particular crate was one of six going to a Mr. T. Schmidt, Malibu CA. Delivery date was the next day, the day of the Surf-O-Rama. Still looking at the paper, I said, "My friends can't compete in the Surf-O-Rama because somebody destroyed their surf-bots and then made sure no other surf-bots were available. This surf-bot and five others like it are to be delivered to a Mr. T. Schmidt, Malibu

CA. Would you care to bet against the T standing for Tankhauser?"

"Not me," said Bill. It occurred to me that Bill could not possibly know what I was talking about.

"If these surf-bots don't show up in Malibu tomorrow, Gotterdammerung won't be able to compete in the Surf-O-Rama either. That'll make things nice and even." I turned to Bill and smiled. I imagined that it looked like the smile on the face of a body that's been dead three days. I don't know what it really looked like. I said, "What if they gave a Surf-O-Rama, and nobody came?"

Bill opened his mouth, about to say something, but I never heard what it was. Lightning flashed in my skull, and then black clouds closed in.

CHAPTER 22
A Family Resemblance

Before I opened my eyes, there was the smell of the ocean. It filled my universe. It was all there was. Then I heard the hiss of gentle waves petting the shore like a lover who couldn't get enough. I lay there on my side for a while, inhaling and listening. Whatever was below me crunched as I breathed. Little crunches, like two crumpled pieces of waxed paper kissing.

I didn't feel bad, or not as bad as I would expect to feel after being sapped. I felt gray and fuzzy, as limp and out of focus as the lint that collects in the screen trap at the back of a clothes dryer. Still without opening my eyes, I touched the back of my head, the place from which the lightning had come. A tender hump back there sent pain along my nerves like rivulets of molten silver.

Then I heard the clicking sound. It seemed impatient. It had been impatient before, in a secret room beneath the SSR building. I opened my eyes a little, squinting against the light of a bright summer day. The ceiling was sky blue, painted with unmoving clouds. I sat up, trying not to be sick. I succeeded, but it was a close contest.

My eyes teared but were able to open a little wider. We were on a beach, or an incredible imitation. It reminded me of the beach diorama at the Daise mansion, but this one was more complete. Instead of looking down on tidal pools and breaking waves, Bill and I were sitting in a sandbox about twenty paces across, from which we looked out at what could almost pass for the Pacific Ocean. I could just see where the sand ended and the painting of beach began. The horizon where the water met the sky was not quite right. The painter had tried, but maybe nobody could get it just right.

Bill stood next to me with a piece of paper attached to the top of his head. On it was the same notice that had been on Bill's head when I'd uncrated him. I pulled it off, and Bill cried, "Look out!" I looked around suddenly, sending more pain zigzagging through my head. Behind me, leaning casually against a big and artistically weathered rock, were three gorillas. They were having a good time watching us.

"Look out!" Tiger squeaked, not sounding much like Bill.

"Shut up," Spike said.

Duke just smiled and pulled a banana from somewhere. He chomped on it, not closing his mouth very much while he did it.

I said, "You guys are still the same fun-loving matched cuff links."

"Huh?" said Tiger.

"Shut up," Spike said.

"I must have blanked out," Bill said.

I said, "You had help," and nodded in the direction of the gorillas. "Meet the Larry, Moe, and Curly of organized crime."

"What kind of crack is that?" said Tiger.

"Shut up," said Spike.

I shook my head—but gently—and said, "You guys need a new writer."

"How about this, then?" Spike said. "We got the Surf-O-Rama all locked up."

"What's that to me?"

"What's that to your friends?" Spike said. "I guess you're not interested in Heavenly Daise anymore, then."

They looked around, suddenly nervous. Even Duke stopped eating. "Nix," said Spike. "Nix."

"That's enough," a new voice said. It was a scratchy voice out of a nightmare. A not-quite-human voice, but carrying baggage that a human would understand. I looked at the spot from where the voice had come. By this time I could see pretty well, and what I saw was worth seeing.

The voice had come from a big lobster as long as both my hands spread out and touching. It paced a little on the rock where it was sitting, the tips of its thin legs making the impatient clicking sound against the hard surface. Its feelers never stopped gently whipping the air. The lobster said, "Get out, the three of you. I want to talk to Marlowe and his 'bot alone."

Spike growled, but Tiger said, "You can't talk like that to us. We're customers."

Spike didn't have a chance to tell Tiger to shut up before the lobster said, "You have your robots, or will soon. I have my money. Our association is at an end. When I say 'Get out,' I mean it."

Duke looked for a place to drop his banana peel, didn't see one he liked, and gloomily tucked it back where he'd gotten it when it was full. He followed

Spike and Tiger through a door that slid open in the wall, ruining the illusion that we were outside, giving the setup all the charm of a plaster cupid. A green wall, the same institutional green that graced the walls at the Malibu police station, was all I could see through the doorway.

"You know, Mr. Daise," I said, "I can see the family resemblance between you and your daughter."

"Is that supposed to be funny, Marlowe?"

"No. Just quick."

Mr. Daise laughed, a millstone grinding exceedingly fine. He said, "The body where I chose to house my intelligence is no business of yours."

"Seems a lot of things are not my business."

"That's right."

"Then I guess I'll be going. Come on, Bill." I didn't move. Neither did Bill.

"Someday you're going to say that once too often." Mr. Daise waved his feelers in the air and tap-danced a little on his rock. Water rolled in from somewhere and then rolled back. Mr. Daise said, "Actually, Marlowe, I wanted to congratulate you on actually finding out where all the surf-bots went. You are a much better detective than I would have guessed."

"Thanks."

"But you found out too late. Those surf-bots are already on their way to Malibu. You can't stop them."

"Too late? You mean Bill and I were knocked out all night?"

"We have ways," Mr. Daise said.

I stood up, just to see if it were possible to stand up. I didn't have brains in my head, but egg yolk. I waited a moment, and I felt better. I took a few steps, and Bill watched me as if he expected me to fall over any moment. He wasn't alone.

I said, "I guess I can stop looking for your daughter now."

"How did you know that?" Mr. Daise asked sharply. Even his feelers stopped waving for a moment.

"Look at the facts. It would be easy for you to find out that I had asked Lance in sales about surf-bots. Maybe he reported anybody who asked about them. It would be logical for you to ask him to do that. Then, when I was caught snooping around your building, you probably got suspicious that mine was not just idle curiosity. You're no dummy, Mr. Daise."

The lobster chuckled and clicked his legs in place. He would have wrung his hands if he'd had any.

"So to distract me from looking into my friends' surf-bot problem, you concocted this story about Heavenly. You know where she is, don't you?"

"No. But her whereabouts are of no particular interest to me as long as she's all right."

"Father-of-the-year material."

Mr. Daise clicked his claws and said angrily, "I've said everything I wanted to say to you, Marlowe. You and your little tin friend, get out."

"It's hard to be really masterful when you're only a lobster, isn't it?"

The waves splashed up behind Mr. Daise while he thought that one over. At last he said, "Say your piece."

"All right. There are a few things I *don't* understand."

"Too bad."

"Sure. Too bad for old Marlowe. But part of what I don't understand might interest you." Mr. Daise said nothing and I went on. "Why is SSR interested in the Surf-O-Rama?"

"It isn't, except insofar as we are protecting our customers, those three gorillas."

"What about Gotterdammerung?"

"Who?"

I'd made a blind shot and hit nothing. I said, "That's the name of a motorcycle gang down at the beach. They seem to be connected with the gorillas."

"Connected in what way?"

"I don't know. But Gotterdammerung takes orders from them. And the gorillas know that I'm working for some surfers out in Malibu who are mighty concerned about the Surf-O-Rama. The chances are good that the gorillas heard who I was working for from Gotterdammerung."

The lobster took a few mincing steps back, as if he were thinking of jumping into the piece of artificial ocean behind him. Bill stood in place, kicking sand backward. He whispered, "Bubble memory ain't enough, is it, Marlowe?"

"Not hardly. Maybe even the right uniform isn't enough." I looked out at the painted horizon and said, "So the gorillas are interested in winning the Surf-O-Rama. They may have encouraged Gotterdammerung to adjust my friends' 'bots with a sledgehammer. Or maybe Gotterdammerung got that idea on their own. It's the kind of idea they'd have."

"Is there something here for me, Mr. Marlowe, or do you just like to compete with the waves?"

"I'm getting to the good part. Ultimately, the whole point of the exercise must be for the gorillas to get Whipper Will's yoyogurt recipe, because that's what the motorcycle maniacs say they want. Do you think maybe those gorillas want to go into business for themselves, Mr. Daise?"

Mr. Daise began, "Look, Marlowe, I have no interest in yoyogurt—"

"Not many lobsters do," Bill said.

I looked down at Bill. I had the sense that Mr. Daise was doing the same thing. I said, "You still need adjustment." Bill didn't say anything but took a few steps up the beach. I said, "What I want to know is, what has all this got to do with Heavenly Daise?"

"You figured that one out yourself. That was just to distract you."

"Sure. Whose idea was it to distract me in that way?"

Mr. Daise didn't say anything for a moment. He didn't move. He might as well have been on a plate surrounded by lemon wedges. Then, slowly, he said, "Spike's."

"I don't think Spike pulled the idea out of a hat."

"Why is that, Marlowe?" Mr. Daise spoke even slower, as if he had to look up each word in a dictionary before he said it.

I sat down on the beach. I'd been standing up a long time, and the bump on the back of my head didn't like it. The dry warm sand felt good. I said, "Because those gorillas aren't just your customers. They're looking for Heavenly. And they've been following me around, hoping I'll lead them to her."

"How do you know?" His voice was still scratchy, but it was so low it mingled with the sound of the surf, making Mr. Daise's words hard to hear.

I said, "They're nice guys. They told me."

"What do they want her for?" Still that same low voice, almost lost in the surf.

I said, "You heard about how the gorillas attacked Sylvia Woods?"

"Well?"

"Well, I have a hunch the gorillas didn't try to kill her because she didn't ask them over for tea. They shot at her because they thought she was Heavenly."

"Impossible."

"Heavenly and Ms. Woods look a lot alike. Especially that evening, when Ms. Woods's hair was arranged like Heavenly's. A lot of folks at Puffy Tootsweet's party made the same mistake."

"You think those gorillas want to kill my daughter?"

"I'm not sure, of course, but that's the way to bet."

The artificial waves beat their heads against the artificial rocks for a long time. The light never changed. It was always high noon there on Mr. Daise's beach. Bill walked down to the water where it swirled between two rocks, and he let his feet get wet. I rocked a little, making an ass-shaped depression in the sand.

Mr. Daise spoke, and I looked up at him. He said, "Get them, Mr. Marlowe. Stop those gorillas any way you can. I have a lot of money. And I know a lot of people downtown."

"I don't kill people if I can help it, Mr. Daise."

"The method is up to you. I just don't want them hurting my little girl."

I stood up. "My method might include cleaning up the little problem I have with surf-bots."

"That doesn't matter to me. I delivered the 'bots. My obligation to the gorillas is at an end. Do whatever seems necessary."

The door slid open, spoiling the illusion again. I walked out with Bill behind me. We walked along the pale green hallway, our footsteps echoing against the metal walls and out an open door.

We walked across a small lot where five little cars with enormous plastic fishtails were parked. We walked out a door at the other side of the lot and instantly were surrounded by crowds of strolling people, none of them in much of a hurry.

"Look at the man with the funny nose, Mommy," a shrill voice said. A child in a pair of red shorts and a T-shirt with the words Mommy's Favorite stamped on it was pointing at me.

"Where the hell are we?" I said.

"Looks like the Oceaneum. A combination tourist trap and fish museum in Santa Monica."

"Let's get out of here."

We hustled through the park, causing only minor disturbances. A guard stopped us at the front gate. He gave me my car keys and told me where my car was parked. Ten minutes later, Bill and I were on our way to Malibu.

CHAPTER 23
Like Father, Like Daughter

Rush hour was over. The air was cool as a mouth full of yoyogurt. I gripped the steering wheel, wanting to drive like a maniac, but I still didn't have a driver's license, and being stopped now would take more time than I had. I concentrated on being the invisible man.

I said, "Loma Alta Vista Del Oro."

Bill tapped the side of his head and said, "I'll let you know when."

The traffic closed up as we approached Whipper Will's house. Enterprising merchants were selling their parking spots—normally free—for three dollars a shot and making it stick. Policemen were everywhere, directing traffic and giving tickets. Casually dressed people were setting up tables along the sidewalk. The Surf-O-Rama would be starting soon. Or it might not. Even I didn't know, though it would all be up to me.

I had to stop at the light in front of Whipper Will's house. More people crossed in front of me, some of them carrying enough equipment to invade a country. One fat guy—wearing a pair of long gray pants, sunglasses, a hat with an orange duck bill, no shirt, and no shoes—was carrying a bag full of burgers, a beach umbrella, an ice chest, a blanket, and a big radio, all by himself. He was good. Somebody had set up a T-shirt store in Whipper Will's parking lot under a big dirty tent that may once have been yellow. I wondered how long that would last.

Behind the parking lot Whipper Will's house was quiet. Of course, the front usually was. Inside, anything could be happening. I wished I were in there doing whatever it was instead of out here trying to even up the Surf-O-Rama score and incidentally trying to prevent a murder. The light turned green, and at the same moment somebody behind me honked. I glided north under the careful eye of a policeman who was sitting in a car parked in a red zone.

Traffic thinned. And soon Bill told me to turn up the hill, away from the ocean. We went up a short, narrow street with bushes crowding in on either side. The bushes had long, sharp leaves and seemed to be attacking with swords as the car pushed past them and they sprang back.

There was a house at the dead end. "Short street for such a long street name," I said. The house had no number, but it had to be the one. We had not passed any others on the way up.

The house was Southern California Spanish, with the obligatory gleaming white stucco walls and terra cotta pantiles on the roof. It was a cozy little bungalow, and not bigger than a palace out of *The Arabian Nights*. A bell hung in each of three tall thin arches near the top of the front wall. The house was a stack of sugar cubes designed like a fortress, just like the Daise mansion. Like father, like daughter.

There was something wrong with the place. I could

not decide what it was, so I pulled the car around in front of the house and turned off the engine. A lot of very excited birds sang in the trees that huddled in on the house, sounding like neurotic jinglebells. If you lived in that house, after a while, you would either stop hearing the noise or you'd have to go bird hunting. Bill put his hand on the door handle and looked at me.

I didn't say anything, but shook my head a little, as if movement cost money. Whoever lived here would know that anybody who came up Loma Alta Vista Del Oro was coming to see them. Somebody might be watching us right now, peeping around a curtain behind one of those windows that was guarded by a fantasy of black wrought iron.

Then I saw what was wrong. It snapped at me the way an optical illusion will snap at you if you stare at it long enough. The trees were fine. The bushes down the driveway were fine. But the bushes that ran along the front of the house looked like plants from T'toom and points east. Some of them looked as if they'd been planted upside down, roots frizzing in the air. Others looked as if they were made of red wax and were half melted to show yellow cores. At least one bush looked more like a vicious animal than any plant had a right to look. Thorns long enough to resemble fangs seemed to gnash in its dragon's mouth. All done in tasteful shades of green.

"Do you see it?" Bill said.

I nodded slowly and said, "If I were their gardener, I'd want a whip and a chair."

I took my water pistol from the glove compartment, wondering what effect a threat of violence would have on a plant. Bill and I got out of the car but stood near it, as if it could protect us. I held the pistol at my side, hiding it from the house with my body, and walked toward the entrance. Bill stayed near me.

The gate into the front patio was painted to match the color of the terra cotta pantiles. It was made of wide boards set at an angle and flush with the front wall. When I took the handle, it made an interesting jiggle but did nothing helpful. I knocked on the door and waited. A fly landed on the back of my neck. I swatted at it, and it went away. A second later, it was back again. I swatted at it again and this time hit a thing like the tip of a wire, which pulled away as I caught it.

I turned suddenly and saw that I was gripping a slim, muscular tendril growing from that vicious-looking plant. The tendril writhed in my hand, and I let go of it. It left a green smear that smelled strongly of freshly cut grass.

The tendril immediately reared back and then launched itself at me. Never in my life have I jumped faster. It was not fast enough. Like a big spring, the tendril coiled itself around me, binding my arms to my sides. I cried out, and Bill tried to pull the tendril loose, but a second tendril snaked out and slapped Bill sharply on the hands. As if he'd been touching a hot stove, Bill leaped back. The tendril was already building a cocoon around me with a network of spidery runners. The plant was absolutely silent and absolutely insistent about wrapping me up.

A tall, golden robot stepped from among the bushes. He looked like the robot in the photograph Mr. Daise had shown me. If Heavenly Daise lived here, he probably was the same one. He was grinning horribly. In a hard but pleasant voice he said, "Don't worry. It likes you."

"Can't we just be friends?" I said.

Bill cried, "Hey!" but without much conviction, as the golden robot gently pushed him out of the way. The big robot took my water pistol; then he casually went through my pockets until he found my wallet. I stood there at attention. The coils were not tight, but awfully alert. If I moved they tightened instantly and stayed tight as long as I struggled.

The golden robot rooted through my wallet while he clicked his tongue. He looked up with surprise and said, "There's nothing in here but a few bucks in cash."

I said, "Of course. I'm a private detective."

"Is that supposed to make sense?"

"Sense or not, that's what I am. Zoot Marlowe. Trouble is my business. This is Bill, my 'bot."

"What do you want?"

"To see Heavenly Daise."

"Who's that?"

I laughed. It was not a polite laugh, but I wasn't feeling polite at the moment.

"If she were here, why would you want to see her?"

"I could tell you her father sent me, but that wouldn't quite be true. He doesn't care where she is."

The robot said, "That sounds like Mr. Daise."

"Yeah. But there are three gorillas who very definitely do care where she is."

The robot stopped smiling. His mouth was a line drawn by a ruler. He tickled along the length of one of the coils. The tendril shuddered and began to loosen. I wriggled out of the coil as the tendril pulled back into the plant. Big thick leaves closed over the teeth, making the plant look no more harmful than a cabbage.

The robot did something with the door handle that I could not see, and the door swung inward. The big golden robot invited me and Bill inside.

As I passed in front of him, I said, "You ought to prune that landscaping before it hurts somebody."

In a long dim corridor, light pressed itself through a thick green awning that was lowered across the archways that opened along one side. The awning made the light green. Walking through the corridor was like walking along the bottom of the ocean. As we walked, I rubbed the palm of my hand on my shirt.

The house's front door was a slab of some blond wood with a peeper eye in the center of it. The robot let us in and led us across a red tile floor to a doorway. It was under a wide carpeted stairway, which led up to the second floor past a single window filled with yellow pebbled glass.

We went down some very narrow and worn wooden stairs to another door, this one like a bank vault.

"Paranoia seems to run in the family," I said.

"The Daises have a lot to be paranoid about," the robot said. He twirled a combination lock. The door chimed. The catch opened with a click, and the door swung aside as if by magic.

We all went through to a big warm room that smelled of chlorine. A wide twin-door refrigerator stood against the wall near a heavy wooden cabinet carved with a lot of baroque dust catchers. Between them was a long table. A glass case ran down its length with some very clean glass jars standing in ranks in-

side. Everything gleamed back and forth at itself in a
self-satisfied way. The entire wall opposite was bank
after bank of dials, switches and meters. Lights
blinked. Back in the corner of the room were a brown
couch and two matching easy chairs, as if someone
had decided the place needed a homey touch and had
broken off a piece of the living room and set it down
here.

Heavenly Daise stood behind a square lab bench
that had a smooth gray stone top. Before her were a
computer screen and keyboard. She finished typing
as we walked in.

Heavenly looked something like Sylvia Woods, but
I convinced myself that there were differences—a
whisker's difference in the length of a nose, an eye-
brow arched into a slightly different curve, lips more
pouty, or less. I could probably tell the two women
apart if they were standing together in a strong light.
If the wind were right and all the planets were in the
right places. Sure I could. Marlowe, master of identi-
fication.

Despite the heat of the day and the warmth of the
room she was wearing a long-sleeved sweater that
looked as if it were knitted from string. The V of the
neckline dived so low I could see most of the tanned
swell of her breasts. Bill walked forward as he said,
"Hey, baby!"

I began, "Bill—" but Heavenly looked at him and
smiled. "Hey, baby," she said.

Bill stopped, a little confused, but he gamely continued, "Let's make it, babe!"

"Get down!" Heavenly said eagerly. "Get funky!"

"Funky?" Bill said.

"Sure," she said. She touched the point of the V on her sweater.

Bill looked at me over his shoulder, a frown on his face that would soon crack the rivets holding his mouth together. He said, "What do I do now?"

"Don't you know?"

Heavenly laughed—a pleasant minor arpeggio. "Of course not. He doesn't have the equipment. For one thing, it isn't made in his size. And like most of the units of his model, he needs a little adjustment. A good dose of reality usually does it."

"You should give that little hint to your sales staff," I said.

Bill walked back to me, his beak nearly shoveling the ground. He said, "How humiliating. I've been adjusted."

"Yeah," I said. "By an expert."

"Who are these bozos?" said Heavenly, idly curious.

The golden robot said, "The one with the nose is Zoot Marlowe, a detective. The little one with the proposition is his 'bot, Bill."

"What do they want?"

"Marlowe mentioned three gorillas."

Heavenly stiffened. She lifted one hand and scratched the opposite arm, but carefully, as if she were petting a cat.

While she was doing that, I said, "Marlowe also knows how to speak English pretty well. He's had lessons."

Heavenly strolled back to the couch, giving us plenty of time to admire how good the tight blue jeans looked on her. She sat down, crossed her legs, and laced her hands around one knee. While the golden robot sat down next to her she said, "All right, Marlowe, speak."

"I need your help."

"What happened to the three gorillas?"

"I'm saving them for the big finish."

"If there is no big finish, Slamma Jamma here will throw you out."

Slamma Jamma, the big golden robot, leaned back and extended his arms along the back of the couch.

"You know about the Surf-O-Rama?"

"For sure," Heavenly said. She cuddled into Slamma Jamma's armpit.

I wondered if it were comfortable to cuddle with something made of metal. What I said was, "Maybe you've heard that SSR has bought all the surf-bots and surf-bot parts along the coast."

"One hears rumors."

"Yeah. One does. One is also threatened by gorillas who were able, despite the disappearance, to purchase a lot of surf-bots from SSR."

"Tell me about the gorillas." Her voice was not as relaxed as her body would have me believe.

"In a minute. First, I want to ask you for some help that would go a long way toward squaring the things SSR has done, and everybody involved with them has done. My friends can't compete in the Surf-O-Rama because somebody, maybe somebody connected in some way with SSR, has worked over their surf-bots, not leaving very much but scrap metal. I'd like you to come with me and even the score by stopping *everybody* from competing."

"That's clever," Heavenly said. "What for?"

"If nobody competes, nobody wins, and nobody loses. Most particularly my friends don't lose a certain bet—involving a special recipe for yoyogurt—they made with some not very wholesome dudes. Who, by the way, also seem to be friends of those gorillas. Interesting, no?"

"I guess I'm supposed to ask, 'Why me?' "

"Because Sylvia Woods says you're a computer genius, and I think that's what it'll take to do the job. This may surprise you, but you're the only computer genius I know."

Bill looked at me as if I'd yanked his head with a chain. I didn't look at him. It got so quiet, I could just about hear the jingling birds outside. Air conditioning hummed.

Heavenly said, "I think it's time for the big finish."

I nodded and said, "Three gorillas are looking for you. That wouldn't mean anything to me except for the fact that they're not very polite about it. Except for the fact that they seem to be involved in the surf-bot chicanery against my clients that I mentioned before. Except for a small matter of attempted murder."

"So?"

"The fact that they are also looking for you involves you in all this to some extent."

"Not much of an extent."

"Maybe not. But your father thinks that it's enough that you need a bodyguard."

"I don't think Slamma Jamma needs help."

I glanced at the big golden robot. He was sitting casually next to Heavenly, one hand resting on one massive leg, his electronic eyes missing nothing. He was casual the way a spider casually waits for flies.

"You may be right. But we still need to talk. Now. First, I need your help. Second, the police will make the same connections I have, and eventually they will find you. I may be able to straighten things out before you have to talk to them."

Heavenly drummed her fingers on Slamma Jamma's leg. Her nails made a noise a lot like the noise her father's feet made on the rocks at his fake seashore. She said, "If anything needs straightening out, Mr. Marlowe, it's you. Obviously, I am not responsible for either the actions of SSR or for whatever some psychotic gorillas may want from me. One of the reasons my father and I take such care with security is that a lot of industrial spies are out there, and some of them are none too gentle."

"You can't think of any reason these particular gorillas might want to see you dead?"

"Nobody has taken a shot at *me*, Mr. Marlowe."

"No. But they've taken a shot at your social secretary, Sylvia Woods."

Heavenly leaned away from Slamma Jamma, and her eyebrows rose just enough. She said, "Why would anybody want to shoot Sylvia?"

"Because," I said, "they thought she was you."

"Reaching, Mr. Marlowe."

"I don't think so. They told me they were looking for you. They shot at her. I'm not reaching very far to make a connection."

Heavenly sighed. It was a great sigh that came from deep within her. "What do you want me to say, Mr. Marlowe? That I know why these three gorillas are after me? That I am somehow involved in a plot to keep surf-bots from your friends? That I have an unnatural interest in yoyogurt?"

"It would be refreshing, yes."

"Mr. Marlowe, when people like you are not bothering me, my life is good. I spend it out here doing the research I want to do. I am looking for better ways to cure warts without surgery, to clear up acne, to banish horrid age spots, prevent ingrown toenails, athlete's foot, and dandruff, to straighten hair and curl hair, to give nose jobs, to improve bustlines and fannies and such."

"To boldly go where no patent medicine has gone before."

"You wound me with your wit," Heavenly said through bared teeth.

Suddenly a two-tone chime began to ring like a doorbell, but insistently and without stopping. Slamma Jamma leaped to his feet, leaving in the cushion where he'd been sitting an impression of concentric circles. He ran across the room to a chart of the human body and pulled a cord next to it. The chart rose, revealing a bank of television screens. We gathered around him as he fiddled with some controls. Each screen showed a view outside the house. In one of them, three men in heavy fur coats, too heavy for the weather, were lumbering away from us as fast as they could go.

CHAPTER 24
Promises, Promises

"They must have followed us," I said.

"Who?" Bill said.

"Those gorillas. And from the speed they're making getting out of here, we'd better do the same." I picked up Bill. I didn't run for the door, but I didn't dawdle either. Slamma Jamma swooped down, picked up Heavenly, and ran ahead of me.

We were out the door in seconds, across the tile, then out the front door. I leaped into the Belvedere and started the engine as Bill leaped into the back seat and Slamma Jamma pushed Heavenly before him into the front. I gunned the engine and roared back down Loma Alta Vista Del Oro. Seconds later the house exploded, blasting bits of wood and plaster and glass against the car with the impact of bullets.

At the bottom of the hill, I stopped before turning left onto PCH. A swift, hot wind blew down at us, carrying the smell of burning wood. We turned and looked out the half-charred rear window. Through the clear part we could see balls of flame boiling up from where the house had been.

"We'd better call the fire department," I said.

Heavenly didn't say anything but turned around to face front. She would never be ugly, but shock made her beauty almost average.

I waited for a hole in traffic and then turned onto PCH, heading back for the surfers' house.

"Is that enough like a shot?" I said angrily. "Do you believe now that those gorillas are after you?"

"I don't understand it," Heavenly said.

"Think it over. Those gorillas didn't choose you at random from the phone book."

I wanted to drive fast, to work off my anger at the gorillas for blowing up the house, at Heavenly for not cooperating, at the whole world for being as nasty as it was. But I was the invisible man. I blended right in with the traffic.

We'd been driving for a while when Heavenly said, "Where are we going?"

"I thought we might look in on the Surf-O-Rama."

"I didn't make you any promises."

"You could promise me now."

Heavenly looked past Slamma Jamma out the window at the ocean. "Surf's up," she said quietly and then did not say anything for a long time. None of us did.

I stopped once, at a burger stand that had a public phone, to call the fire department. Traffic began to back up. There was a lot of honking and fast lane-changing, but nothing would get you where you were going any faster. Some people kept trying anyway. The police had to deal with a few of them.

The tables that people had been setting up earlier had now become concessions selling junk jewelry, brass doodads, fast food, T-shirts, pennants, binoculars, paintings done on velvet. They lined the street for miles. Not even the constant breeze off the beach could blow away the smells of cooking grease and incense. Colorfully dressed people grazed among the tables, buying things they would never buy at home. What didn't make them sick would make them wonder tomorrow why they'd bought it today.

Eventually I drew up to the tiny parking lot outside the surfers' house. The lot was empty. As I'd guessed, Whipper Will must have chased away the T-shirt people with the dirty yellow tent. As I pulled in, a policeman started over to us. But when he saw that I had a key to the house, he went back to holding up a telephone pole and interrogating a thin woman who was mainly wearing some blond hair that fell in waves to the bottom of her bottom.

Nobody was home. I herded Heavenly, Slamma Jamma, and Bill through the house to the kitchen and out the back door. People moved up and back on the black paved strip either afoot, or on bicycles or roller skates. Classical music bobbed and feinted with rock-and-roll as people carrying radios passed. The blues swung in and out. There were a lot of dogs, on leashes and off. At least one woman in a bright red next-to-nothing had a live snake draped around her neck. Beyond the strip, you could not see the beach for the people. Whipper Will and the others were out there someplace. Probably as close to the water as they could manage. They wouldn't be able to stay away, even if they couldn't compete.

I said, "Excuse me," and got two kids to move so that I could stand on the wall between the backyard and the public strip. This put me almost eye to eye with Slamma Jamma. Now I could see a line of surf-bots out on the water, their arms outstretched and leaving trails of colored smoke from their fingers.

"Look over there," I said. I pointed a little to one side, where a judges' stand had been built from wood and a lot of red-white-and-blue bunting. In front of it, Gotterdammerung was checking things on some shiny new surf-bots. I thought of cockroaches nibbling at silver sardines.

"I never promised," Heavenly said.

"Sure. I know. Let those gorillas get away with everything. It's OK."

"What would you want me to do?"

"Forget it," I said sharply and waited.

"No, really," Heavenly said.

I sighed. I made it seem as if explaining things to Heavenly would be the most difficult thing I'd ever done, at least that week. I said, "See those people in black down there, setting up their 'bots?"

"Yes."

"That's Gotterdammerung. I think they work for the gorillas. I think that if they win, the gorillas will win."

"What do you want me to do?"

I still wasn't looking at her. I said, "I want you to jam Gotterdammerung's remote-control boxes."

"Why?"

"I want to test a little theory."

I glanced at Heavenly. She was looking at Gotterdammerung, nodding. She said, "I don't have any equipment."

Bill said, "I'll bet Slamma Jamma has a lot of swell circuits inside him."

Heavenly shrugged and said it was worth a try. She asked Slamma Jamma for his tool kit. He opened a door in his hip and handed her a slim plastic packet. Then, at Heavenly's request, he lay down on the red bricks in the backyard and spread his legs a little. Heavenly knelt between his legs and, with a finger-nail, opened a long door down the inside of the big muscle above the knee. A bank of tiny lights—red, green, and blue—flashed above screws and switches mice might use to turn their lights on and off.

From the slim packet Heavenly took slim tools and began to adjust things inside Slamma Jamma's leg. Slamma Jamma groaned once or twice, and his right arm twitched. A moment later, Heavenly sat back on her heels and said, "I'm about done."

"All right." Out on the water, Tankhauser and a tall blond guy wearing a blue windbreaker and yellow walking shorts stood on the contestants' platform watching their 'bots swim out. The 'bot the other guy was running had been painted with black and red ti-ger stripes. As soon as Tankhauser's silver 'bot stood up and began his ride, I said, "Do it now."

Heavenly threw a tiny mouse switch. Nothing hap-pened. The silver 'bot continued to cruise through the tube, keeping up pretty well with the other 'bot.

"I thought it might not work," Heavenly said.

"I thought so too," I said. "Why don't you give it a try, Bill?"

"My meat," Bill said and scrambled down between Slamma Jamma's legs as Heavenly got to her feet. Bill studied the electronics for a moment, then went to work.

Heavenly watched him until the two 'bots slid onto the beach on their boards. The next heat would begin soon. Behind us, Bill scratched around on the bricks as he moved. Heavenly said, "I guess Sylvia was wrong about my being a computer genius."

"Maybe."

She looked at me sharply, then decided not to ask me what the hell I meant by that. Her face softened into a gentle smile. "Bill is a good little 'bot."

"Good enough so far," I said.

She agreed and a moment later, Bill said, "I got it."

Heavenly grunted. Maybe it was supposed to be a cynical laugh, but it sounded like a grunt.

Wortan lumbered up the three steps onto the contestants' platform. He'd worked white ribbons into his hair and beard. He was as cute as a rusty screen door. He nodded to the kid who stood next to him. The kid was not much taller than I, and he wore an orange wet suit. He threw back his head and cried, "Ahhroooh!" and the crowd cheered, momentarily overwhelming the sound of the waves. Wortan put one big mitt on the kid's shoulder but took it away immediately.

Wortan's 'bot was the same silver as Tankhauser's, but white ribbons were tied around its wrists and ankles. The kid's 'bot was orange, like his wet suit. They swam out. A big wave rolled in, and the two 'bots stood up.

"Now," I said.

Bill said, "You got it." For a moment, the orange 'bot did a crazy dance, then it stood at attention and went down with its board. Wortan's ribbon-bedecked 'bot hung ten and went into a Quasimodo pose, sailing along like a marble on glass.

I said, "I think that those 'bots Gotterdammerung are running aren't any more remote-controlled than

I am. I think somebody ought to tell the judges about it. What do you think?"

"Was that your little theory?" Heavenly said.

"Part of it."

"What's the other part?"

I was going to tell her what the other part was, but I didn't have a chance. Three gorillas stepped around the side of the house. Each of them was wearing a blue bathing suit, a yellow tank top, and a pair of mirror shades. What improved their appearance even less was the fact that each of them was pointing a pistol in our direction.

CHAPTER 25
More or Less Human

I could have been a hero. I could have led Heavenly
and the others away while the three gorillas shot us
in our backs. I could have jumped at the three of them,
knocked their heads together, and eaten their pistols
like licorice. But I wasn't a hero. I was just some guy
from T'toom doing his best to play a game that had
gotten rougher than even my father or Grampa Zamp
could have guessed. Be careful, my father had told me.
If he could see me now.

Slamma Jamma stood up. Heavenly backed into
him, and he closed his arms around her. She stuck
her tongue between her teeth like a little girl concentrating, and her face was so white above Slamma Jamma's mountainous arms that it seemed like a face
drawn on an egg.

Spike said, "It's been a long time, honey." He used
the kind of growl that usually comes from the back of
a dark cave. "We're gonna go inside now and catch
up on things." The three walked forward, backing us
into the house.

No one was looking in our direction. Two kids who
weren't watching the surfing were mighty involved in

each other. I could have shouted and attracted some attention, but I didn't want to be clever around three not-very-bright guys with guns.

They backed us through the kitchen and into the living room. As usual, the curtains were closed. Nobody could see us now. We stood in the center of the room like a gaggle of penguins on an ice floe.

Heavenly said, "If you guys are the same ones who crashed Puffy Tootsweet's party, it hasn't been a long time. Not long enough, anyway." Her voice was grim, and it shook a little.

Spike said, "At Puffy Tootsweet's party we shot the wrong dame by mistake. This time there ain't no mistake."

Tiger chuckled and Spike told him to shut up.

Heavenly made a jittery laugh. It was weak, and it knew it was weak. She said, "Is wishful thinking the only kind of thinking you guys do? I'm still not Heavenly Daise. I'm Sylvia Woods." She grabbed the shoulder of her bulky sweater, and with a hard yank tore it open. Under all that bulk were bandages very much like the ones Sylvia had been wearing when I'd driven her home from the emergency room.

Spike looked at Duke. Duke shrugged. Tiger said, "Let's cream her no matter who she is."

I said, "That's what I like about you, Tiger. Once you set your mind on a thing you couldn't lift it off with a crane."

"You both shut up," Spike said. In a quieter, less certain voice, he said, "I'm thinking."

"This oughta be good," I said. Spike said, "Shut up" again, a little hysterically, I thought. He waved the gun in my direction.

We were all quiet for a while. Early afternoon sun

struggled to get through the heavy curtains. Dust fell. Outside, people cheered as robots rode the ocean on boards. Music came and went as people walked by with radios. Traffic grumbled on Pacific Coast Highway. More dust fell. We were still quiet.

"All right," I said. "Just for a minute, let's assume that this is Sylvia Woods. Would you mind telling her why you want Heavenly Daise?"

"Sure. No problem. I been turning it over in my mind for so long it's shiny and worn from handling. I want to show it to somebody."

I said, "That's good, Spike. I could have said that."

"Yeah," he growled. "And you probably will some day."

While Duke and Tiger kept us covered, Spike pointed the pistol at me, but for the moment it was not a pistol. It might have been his finger he shook in my face. He took a confidential tone, as if it were just him and me sitting on stools in a bar somewhere. An almost friendly voice talking about what happened at the office that day. But there was an edge to the voice that made me think of straitjackets and padded rooms. He said, "You know what kind of work Heavenly Daise was doing?"

"Some kind of genetic manipulation, Sylvia told me."

"That's what Heavenly told us too when we answered the ad in the paper. And then she told us she was looking for a way to grow hair on bald men. Can you imagine?"

Without waiting for me to answer, he went on. "Me and Duke and Tiger, we gave blood before, so we weren't afraid of no needles. And Heavenly Daise was offering a lot more money than the blood people."

Heavenly's expression was fixed. She was looking in Spike's direction, but I couldn't tell whether she was watching him, or looking back in time, or maybe at nothing at all.

"To do what?" I said, hoping that I hadn't already guessed.

"To manipulate our genes," Spike said in a voice hard enough to cut diamonds. But he wasn't excited. He was just telling a story. He went on in the same even tone but with the air of a man coming to the punch line. "And you know what? She manipulated our genes so good that she not only grew hair on our heads, but all over us." He smiled, showing broad, flat, crooked teeth.

"You mean you guys are human?" I said.

"More or less," Spike said. He began to laugh. Tiger saw that laughing was OK and began to do it with him. They laughed hard and a little crazy, like men who'd waited a long time to do it. Duke smiled, but his pistol never wavered.

The laughter slowed, sounding like an engine running down. Spike and Tiger looked at each other and set themselves off again, but by that time the laughter was forced and a little stale. Heavenly hadn't moved since Spike had begun to tell his story. She wasn't moving now. Slamma Jamma stood near her but not touching her. Bill shuffled in place between me and Slamma Jamma.

When Spike and Tiger stopped laughing again, I said, "You could have gone to the police. There are laws about experimenting on people."

Duke spoke now in a voice so heavy it had trouble leaving his mouth. We had to listen hard. He said, "We don't want justice. We want revenge."

Heavenly shivered.

"But this isn't Heavenly," I said.

"It don't matter," Spike said, explaining things to the dunce. "We gotta kill her, just to be sure. We gotta kill all of youse 'cause you're witnesses."

"Sure. A day without murder is like a day without sunshine."

"Sorry, shamus. I was just beginning to like you." He aimed his pistol at me. Duke held tight on Heavenly. Tiger pointed at Slamma Jamma. The moment hung there like the tip of a slaberingeo's tail at the top of its arc, just before it drops and one of its spikes nails you to the ground.

CHAPTER 26
Gorillas and Friends of Gorillas

Heavenly groaned softly. Too late I remembered my water pistol. Even later than that, I remembered that Slamma Jamma had taken it away from me and not given it back. It was probably gone with the house.

With a single smooth motion Slamma Jamma's chest opened down the center on hinges and twin cannons popped from inside. They shot quickly and recoiled as they shot. The explosive noise was so loud it blew out windows in the living room and in the kitchen. Slamma Jamma continued to fire. Shells pummeled each of the gorillas, as if invisible birds were pecking them to death as they fell. The firing mechanism continued to click into the crashing silence long after the shells were gone.

"You can stop now," I said as screams came from outside, and a hand pushed a curtain aside to let a round, serious face with a bush of dark hair look into the room and say, "What's shaking?" Far away, sirens began to wail. They got closer.

I could hear a crowd gathering outside. More faces looked in, their number growing in a cluster, like soap bubbles. The faces didn't mean anything to me. I sat down on a nearby chair and Bill squatted next to me. Slamma Jamma helped Heavenly to the couch. She fell back onto it stiffly. Deftly, with the calm assurance of a man buttoning his shirt, Slamma Jamma pushed the cannons back into his chest and closed the doors. He said, "She needs some water."

"In the kitchen," I said. There was nothing in my head but relief. I looked at the three dead gorillas. They were just three dead gorillas. They meant no more to me than the pile of big dirty pillows they'd fallen on.

There was pounding on the front door and deep urgent shouts: "Open up! It's the police." I dragged myself to my feet and went to open the door before they knocked it down. I opened the door, and three young policemen stood there, hands on holsters. One of them said, "We heard shooting."

"Right the first time," I said. "Come on in." They herded me down the hall and back into the living room. One of them immediately knelt next to the gorillas while the others looked around the room, mainly watching us.

One of them said, "What went on here?"

I said, "Those three were going to murder us. Slamma Jamma there shot back in self-defense."

The officer on the floor looked as if he'd eaten something that didn't agree with him. He said, "These birds are dead. Good and dead by the number of holes in them."

"Birds." I made a short sharp laugh.

Whipper Will ran into the room from the kitchen, followed by Captain Hook and the others. "Cowabunga," Whipper Will said as he looked around.

"Who are you?" a policeman said.

"This is our hang." When Whipper Will saw no comprehension on the policeman's face, he said, "We live here," as if that should have been obvious.

The sound of angry engines drowned out the policeman's next question, and a second later Tankhauser, still mounted on his hog of a motorcycle, rolled into the room leading his gang, also on motorcycles. Hardware, noise, and evil-smelling smoke filled the room.

Tankhauser revved his engine and shouted over the noise, "Hey, look! Surf shit shot the boss!" Then he saw the three policemen. The delighted smile that had been under construction on his face fell back into a tangled wreckage. He tried to bully his gang out of there, but there wasn't much room to turn a motorcycle, and besides that, by this time there were more policemen at the back door.

The police arrested everybody in the house. Except the gorillas, of course. They were past arresting, or anything else.

The wagon came and took us to the Malibu police station.

It was late, and it felt late, but it was also summer so light was just fading from the sky. I was sitting in the wooden chair that had cigarette burns on the arms, looking across an ancient green-topped desk at Sergeant Faraday. Faraday looked at me, pulled his lower lip, then ran a hand through the brush that grew from his head.

We had all spent some time giving fingerprints and statements. Robots gave their serial numbers. If the police didn't just stick my prints into a file, but had an expert look at them, they would get a surprise.

I had been at the police station for a long time and was beginning to feel as if I belonged there. It was not a feeling I liked. When Faraday went into his routine again, I said, "If you're doing that for my benefit, you can stop."

Faraday took his hand down and said, "I told you we'd find those gorillas, but I don't guess I'll shove them down your throat."

"No. Seeing as how I delivered them to you on a platter."

"Yeah. Them and fourteen other assorted geeks and gimcracks. Plus two robots, one very expensive, the other one less so."

"What are you going to do with them?"

Faraday blew through pursed lips, and just to keep in practice, combed his hair again. He said, "We got hold of the control boxes those motorcycle maniacs were using on their surf-bots. They were empty, so you were right about the 'bots surfing under their own control. Maybe Bunco will have something to say about that. But we have them for crashing Puffy Toot-sweet's party and destroying property there. Tres-passing and vandalism at the very least."

"My guess is that they are not new at crashing and destroying."

"You're a genius, Marlowe."

"Yeah. Anything in the fact that they admitted in the presence of three police officers that they worked for the gorillas?"

"Look, Marlowe, we don't think a whole hell of a lot of those creeps ourselves. But we gotta check on things before we hang somebody. They'll get the same breaks as anybody else. Got that?"

"Good enough. What about the big robot that shot the gorillas?"

"Self-defense. Or defense of his owner, anyway. And the rest of them are just surfers who happened to live in the house. Surfing isn't a criminal offense yet. A couple of them have outstanding parking tickets." Faraday shrugged. Then he looked at me with his eyebrows up. "Anything else you'd care to tell us about those gorillas?"

"They were looking for Heavenly Daise, and they found her."

"Looking why?"

"Is it important?"

"I guess not. Not for the files, anyway."

I stood up and said, "Anything else?"

"Where are you from, Marlowe?"

I smiled and walked out. A police car had already taken the surfers home. In the lobby I met Heavenly, Bill, and Slamma Jamma. Heavenly said, "I spoke to my father. He wants to talk to you."

"Fine," I said. "That'll make it easier for me to talk to him."

One of the three young policemen who'd been at the scene of the shooting drove us back to the surf house. He kept looking at us, but he didn't say anything. None of us did. When he dropped us off, he wished us luck and drove away.

We got into my car, and I took us to Hollywood.

CHAPTER 27
One Aggro Dude

We did not speak much during the ride, each of us having his own thoughts. The air was warm and soft, and it made the world seem warm and soft too.

I drifted along with the traffic, trying to stay out of trouble. Only cars behind the Chevy seemed to be in much of a hurry. They kept swinging around me angrily, getting in front of me, and then deciding they had some time to rubberneck after all. I loved California drivers who wanted to prove in their own dangerous way that *I* was a terrific driver.

When we got to the Daise mansion it was nearly dark, and the place seemed wrapped in gray flannel. Nobody had to push the buzzer at the gate. It opened as we approached. We were expected.

I pulled up next to the big car that Heavenly never drove. We walked to the door, and Davenport let us in. He welcomed Heavenly home and said, "Good evening" to me. Slamma Jamma and Bill were so much dead weight to him. They got all the respect due a piece of luggage.

Davenport hurried to the library where I'd first met Sylvia Woods and opened the door for us. We went in, and he closed the door gently behind us. We stood in the center of the room in a small confused clump. Heavenly said, "That Davenport needs a good cleaning. My father isn't in here."

"Yes, I am," said a voice. It was the scratchy nightmare voice. Only it was too familiar to give me bad dreams now. I looked in the direction of the voice and saw a shallow stainless steel pan on a desk. In the pan was Mr. Knighten Daise, still looking a lot like a lobster.

Heavenly took a step forward and craned her neck at the lobster as if she were looking over a wall. "Dad?" she said in a very uncertain voice.

"Who else would it be?" he said.

She looked at me as if I would know and said, "Is this some kind of joke?"

"Don't you recognize me?" the lobster said and laughed like corduroy pants laughing.

"It *is* a joke," Heavenly said and crossed her arms. She sat down on the long leather couch. Slamma Jamma moved in to stand behind her. When he stood still like that, his face impassive, he looked like the piece of machinery he was.

"No joke, cutes," Mr. Daise said. Coming from a lobster, it sounded obscene. He went on, "I have a lot of enemies. Even more than you have, and evidently you have plenty. I needed to disappear. But there was work to do, and I couldn't really go away. So I had my brain put into this lobster body. You might want to do the same. I'll give you the number of my surgeon."

Heavenly shuddered and said, "Keep it."

The room was silent but for the ticking of the clock. Mr. Daise said, "Can I get any of you a brandy?"

Heavenly looked away. Bill opened his mouth to

say something but squatted next to me and said nothing. I said, "No thanks, Mr. Daise. I was told you wanted to see me."

"Can't we be civilized about this?" Mr. Daise said. He reached a foot out of the pan and touched one of a rack of buttons. A moment later, Davenport entered the room. Mr. Daise said, "Brandy." Davenport took a square bottle from a sideboard and carefully poured brown fluid into the metal pan. Mr. Daise wriggled in the brown fluid and made lip-smacking sounds. I don't know how he did that without lips. Davenport put the bottle away, then went out and closed the door.

Mr. Daise said, "It seems you were correct about those gorillas, Mr. Marlowe. If it hadn't been for Slamma Jamma, they would have killed Heavenly. What I want to know is *why* they wanted her dead."

"Ask Heavenly."

Heavenly turned toward the bookshelf as if one of the books had called her name.

"I'm asking *you*, Marlowe. You're the detective. Report."

"You hired me to find your daughter, Mr. Daise. There she is, and not damaged much. But I'll tell you anyway because you'll need to know."

"Go on."

"Those gorillas wanted to see Heavenly dead because of a genetic experiment she did on them. They were a little upset that they were men she'd made into monkeys, and they wanted their revenge."

Mr. Daise waved his feelers in Heavenly's direction and said, "I told you that genetics stuff would get you into trouble."

"The family business bores me," Heavenly said without looking at the lobster.

"Kids," Mr. Daise said as he beat the brandy with his legs. He didn't stop when he said, "OK. We know the gorillas asked me to hire you to distract you from finding out what happened to all the surf-bots. And incidentally to really find Heavenly. Was there anything for them in the surf-bot angle?"

"As it turns out, that has a lot to do with Heavenly too."

Heavenly turned slowly to look at me. She didn't like me so much now. I had the feeling that she would like me less as time went on.

I said, "It's kind of complicated, but I'll start with this. Sylvia Woods and Heavenly Daise are the same woman."

"A lot of people make that mistake," Mr. Daise said.

"No mistake. For one thing, there is that little matter of Heavenly's injured arm. Very much like the injury Sylvia got from the gorillas at Puffy Tootsweet's party."

Heavenly nodded and said, "Dumb luck."

"Oh, that was just the clincher," I said. "I could have guessed that you and Sylvia were the same woman even without dumb luck."

"Talk, Marlowe," Heavenly said with all the warmth of a snake reminding a hamster it was feeding time.

"First there is the matter of Slamma Jamma. When he stood up at Heavenly's beach house—now deceased—he left an impression on the couch. It was the same set of concentric circles I saw on this very couch here the day I spoke to Sylvia Woods for the first time."

"So?"

"So, maybe you'd have another robot of the same

model kind of like wandering around your house. I'd prefer to believe that it was Slamma Jamma because that's the simplest explanation. You'll like this next part, Mr. Daise, because it speaks well of your company."

"Make it march," Mr. Daise commanded, barking as best he could without a barker.

"You call your company Surfing Samurai Robots because your robots are built to be entirely loyal to their owners. I figure that's true of Slamma Jamma as much as for any other SSR robot. Why would he be in this house if Heavenly wasn't here? If Heavenly had been here, chances are good that Sylvia would have known about it. She didn't mention it. Is it too far for you to leap that Sylvia, who looks just like Heavenly, really *is* Heavenly? On the other hand, why would Slamma Jamma be at the beach house guarding Sylvia, who wasn't there?"

"Circumstantial," Heavenly said. "And a cheap shot."

"Maybe. But I have more evidence. For one thing, Heavenly, who is supposed to be an electronics genius, wasn't able to jam the signals that the Surf-O-Rama contestants were using to control their 'bots, even though Bill here had no trouble. I had to figure that was because she didn't really want to jam them."

"And why is that, Marlowe?" Heavenly said.

"Because you wanted Gotterdammerung to win."

"But Gotterdammerung wasn't really controlling their 'bots. What difference would it make whether I jammed signals or not?"

"You saw what happened when Bill jammed them."

Heavenly took a deep breath and let it out slowly.

Mr. Daise said, "Why would Heavenly care who won the Surf-O-Rama?"

"Because if Gotterdammerung won, she'd get Whipper Will's yoyogurt recipe."

"Whose what?" Heavenly said. She didn't like me at all, but at least I had her interest.

I said, "That's OK, Ms. Daise. I like to talk. It's this way: That laboratory of yours is set up like a fancy version of Whipper Will's back room, the place where he makes his yoyogurt. There's the refrigerator and the warm box and the clean glassware. And the place smells like the chlorine you use to keep stray un-wanted bacteria from growing. How am I doing so far?"

"You interest me strangely." She walked to the sideboard and got herself a brandy. She didn't swim in it but poured it into a whiskey glass and knocked it back all at once. She panted for a moment and shook her head. "Please go on," she said, her voice strained through the liquor.

"So, because of the setup, I figured you were inter-ested in yogurt, if not yoyogurt. Maybe it even had something to do with your genetic research."

"Reaching," Heavenly said.

"Yes? What about those horror movie plants you have growing around your house?"

"I'm not the gardener," Heavenly said.

"No, but you had to get rid of bad batches of yo-yogurt somehow. Batches that were potent genetic manipulators but that didn't do what you wanted them to do. If you were a good citizen and didn't put it down the drain and into the public water system, maybe you just dumped the stuff out a window onto some unlucky bushes that grew a little strange from then on."

"It won't work, Marlowe. You know yourself that Gotterdammerung was working for the gorillas. Gotterdammerung was not working for me. If they had been, they'd have said something at the surfers' house or in the paddy wagon."

"It's true. Tankhauser isn't the kind of guy to keep it to himself when he knows somebody—especially somebody he thinks might be able to help him stay out of jail."

"So," said Heavenly, constructing her case carefully, "if I really was interested in yoyogurt, and I was going to get it because Gotterdammerung won the Surf-O-Rama, then Gotterdammerung would have to give it to the gorillas, and the gorillas would have to give it to me."

"That's right," I said, walking into her trap with my eyes open.

With a note of triumph, Heavenly said, "You can't have it both ways, Marlowe. Either I hired the gorillas so I could get the yoyogurt or I didn't. If I hired them, why didn't they shoot me on the spot? More to the point, why would I hire somebody I knew had a grudge against me?"

"My guess is that the gorillas traced you to Malibu and that they found you in *Sylvia* mode. You saw your chance to use them to get yoyogurt and hired them. *Sylvia* mode can be pretty convincing. I ought to know. If you hadn't worn your hair like Heavenly that one time at Puffy Tootsweet's party, you'd have come out of this without a scratch."

"But—" she began.

"And," I steamrolled over her, "you said more than

once that all gorillas looked alike to you. It's a funny thing to say. I don't know why you'd think there might be another set of gorillas in the world that wore suits."

"I'm not the only one doing genetic research," she said in a voice that came back not quite far enough from the dead.

"Yes, yes," Mr. Daise said impatiently. "You say Heavenly is Sylvia. She and I will talk about that. You say Heavenly hired gorillas to help her get yoyogurt. Why didn't she buy the surf-bots herself? She could have gotten the company discount."

"You're such a fool, Dad," said Heavenly as she poured another drink. "You know as well as I do that if you'd known I wanted to use surf-bots to get yoyogurt, you would have stopped the sale. We all know what you think of my genetic experiments."

I laughed, not because it was funny, but because it was sad. I said, "Someday, you're going to have to climb over that wall between you—if only to see what's on the other side."

Mr. Daise stopped moving his feelers. Most of the brandy in his pan was gone. He spoke carefully when he said, "So the gorillas played all of us for suckers. They didn't care anything about yoyogurt or about the Surf-O-Rama. They just wanted to find Heavenly."

"Right," I said. "They had me look for her, hoping I'd do the job they couldn't do. If I succeeded, they were all right. If I failed, they didn't lose anything, not even my fee, because SSR was paying the bill."

Mr. Daise said, "But why did the gorillas bother to hire that motorcycle gang to surf against the surfers?"

Heavenly said, "Because, I suppose, surfers and motorcycle gangs are traditional enemies. At least in the old surfing movies. Motorcycle gangs surfing against surfers would look less suspicious than gorillas surfing against surfers. Look, Zoot, if Gotterdammerung had their way, they'd have beaten the surfers with tire irons. Give me a little credit for ordering the gorillas not to hurt anybody or let anybody get hurt."

"A little credit," I said flatly. "You didn't kill anybody or have anybody killed, except indirectly. I guess that makes you a big hero."

Mr. Daise said, "She tried to fix the Surf-O-Rama. Is that so bad?"

"Not so bad as some other things I could name. But if she promised not to do it again, I'd feel better. It would get me off a hook I'm on."

"I have important work to do," Heavenly said.

"That justifies everything, I suppose." I stood up. "Look," I said, "next time either of you needs a detective, talk it over with the other and then call somebody else."

Mr. Daise pushed his button again. Heavenly sipped her drink. Davenport came in, and Mr. Daise told him to show me out.

"Come on, Bill," I said. We beat Davenport to the front door, and I opened it myself. It was something. Not much, but something.

I had solved the entire mystery except for one small part of it. Maybe that part didn't matter at all to anybody except me, but that was enough. I counted. I'd worked to get the answer, and I would get it.

The tables and hawkers and tourists were gone from along Pacific Coast Highway. The road had shed the glitter and the bangles and was itself again instead of a circus midway.

I parked and went into the house with Bill. We walked through the house to the kitchen. There was still no glass in the windows, but that didn't matter much on a mild night like this. Most of the surfers were out on the beach playing Frisbee by the light of torches that stuck out of the sand at angles like drunken trees.

I found Whipper Will and Bingo in the living room sitting on the floor in front of the couch not watching something on television. A guy with a nose almost as long as mine was leaping around with a sword and talking louder than he had to.

I sat down in a chair across from them and watched Bingo and Whipper Will paw each other.

I said to Bill, "They're a cute couple, aren't they?"

"Cuter than a greasy biscuit."

"Is the swift dialogue part of the programming too?"

"Sort of. Each of us is supposed to take on the personality of our master."

"I have a lot to answer for," I said.

Whipper Will and Bingo came out of their clinch, and Whipper Will said, "They're still trying to decide what to do about the Surf-O-Rama. Everybody's pretty ripped about it. If Gotterdammerung shows up on the beach again, it'll be a pretty grotty scene. And, oh, yeah. The guy is coming tomorrow to put new glass in the windows."

"Sorry about the glass."

"It's cool. I figure it's part of the cost of cleaning up the beach. What's shaking by you?"

I told him, trying not to incriminate Heavenly Daise too much. When I was done, Bingo whistled one long low note, and Whipper Will said, "You're an aggro dude, Zoot."

"Yeah. Me and your Aunt Edith. There's just one thing I want to know. I almost got killed a couple of times defending it, and I deserve to know it. What's so special about yoyogurt?"

Whipper Will made mystic passes through the air and said in a stagey voice, "Nobody knows."

I didn't laugh. I didn't smile. I just waited, my fingers drumming on the arm of the chair. The curtains moved gently in the breeze, as if the ghosts of old surfers were passing in and out.

Whipper Will put his hands down and sent Bingo for a brewski. He told her to take her time. She went without a glance back. When she was gone, Whipper Will said, "It's true. Nobody knows."

"You fascinate me strangely," I said, remembered where I'd heard it, and wished I hadn't.

"A lot of yogurt is made with artificial colors and flavors and preservatives. I use the stuff from my garden. It's entirely natural."

"That can't be all. I've eaten fruit. It doesn't have that kind of punch."

Whipper Will looked down and shook his head. He said, "For the rest of it, I really *don't* know except for this: The bacterium in yoyogurt is some kind of new strain, a mutation or something, that I discovered by accident. I just culture it and let it work."

I thought about that for a moment, and then said, "What about you, Will?"

"Me?" He glanced in the direction of the kitchen. Bingo was still getting the brewski.

"Yeah. You have a brain between your ears, and

you even use it sometimes. What are you doing out here at the beach?"

He looked me straight in the eye and said, "Where are you from, Zoot?"

I smiled. Whipper Will smiled back. We were still at it when Bingo came back with two brewskis. Whipper Will took a swallow from his can and said, "Thanks, dude, for all your help. Philip Marlowe would be proud."

I thanked him and went out of the room feeling that he was right. I really had done a good job, and I knew it. I was a good enough man for this world, anyway. As for who Whipper Will was or where he came from, each of us has a right to some secrets.

I stood for a while at the back door watching surfers throw around a plastic thing that looked a lot like the ship waiting for me under the Pacific Ocean.

Bill came up next to me and said, "Lot of stars out tonight."

I looked up, tried to find T'toom's sun among the pricks of light, and failed. I said, "Yeah." A moment later, I shook off my melancholy and ran out to join the surfers.